CONTENTS

CHAPTER		PAGE
1	Pursued by a Wolfpack	2
2	Showdown with a She-Wolf	22
3	A Mate and a Lair	42
4	Through the Wall of Light	64
5	Captured!	78
6	The Loss of a Mother	90
7	The Return of a Runaway	102
8	In the Service of Man	112
9	The Enemy of His Kind	132
10	The Misnamed Master	140

11   Rescue and Release   166

12   The Triumph of Love   184

13   Good-bye to the Yukon   198

14   Learning a New Life   214

15   Guarding of the House   236

CHAPTER 1

Pursued by a Wolfpack

Human beings can adapt themselves to various climates and living conditions. People live in deserts and jungles, on the banks of flooding streams, and in mountainous regions. They live in places where snow and bitter cold are almost always present.

Using their wits, people learn how to handle the dangers of their climate. They develop the kind of clothing that will protect them from freezing temperatures or the hot sun. If there are deadly animals nearby, they learn how to avoid them or, if necessary, to kill them.

If we live in a land of comfort and security, it may be difficult to appreciate what it is like to dwell under conditions such as those described above. We must simply use our imaginations to put ourselves in those strange settings.

If you are ready to do that, then imagine a land covered by deep snow as far as one can see in every direction. A land where the temperature reaches fifty degrees below zero. A land lying in darkness much of the time, with the sun shining only briefly. A land where animals run wild and only a few human beings can be found. A land where silence is the rule, rather than the noises of people and their machines.

So silent and so wild is this land near to the chill Arctic Ocean that it may be properly called "the Wild." Let us go back almost a century and see what kinds of things could happen in the snow and the silence.

The sound of sled dogs broke the silence. There were six of them, yipping and panting as they pulled their sled. The fur on their bodies was covered with frost. As their breath left their nostrils, it froze and formed a coating of ice crystals around their heads and necks.

They had names given to them by their human masters. Some of those names described an unusual feature that a particular dog possessed. One was called One Ear for an obvious reason. Another was named Fatty. Then there was Frog, whose bark sounded like the croaking of a frog.

Each dog wore a leather harness. The dogs were connected to one another and to the sled by leather traces, or lines. They combined their efforts to pull a heavy load over the soft snow.

The sled they pulled was made of bark from the birch tree. It had no runners, but lay fully on the surface of the snow. It carried the normal items that men would need in the Wild: blankets, an axe for cutting firewood, a coffeepot, and a frying pan.

5

There was also a more unusual piece of cargo on the sled. A long, narrow wooden box held the body of a man. Lord Alfred had died here in the Wild while searching for gold. His body was being transported to Fort McGurry, which was still miles away.

Two other men, still very much alive, drove the sled and the dogs toward their destination. Their names were Bill and Henry, and they looked like twins as they worked the dogs. Each had covered his body with as much fur and soft leather as possible. They had to keep their flesh safe from the bitter, dangerous cold. Of course, their faces could not be completely covered. They had to be able to see and, when necessary, to cry out to the dogs and to one another. Their exposed eyelashes and cheeks and lips were coated with ice crystals, so they looked somewhat like twin ghosts.

They worked in silence, speaking only when they had to. In the Wild many dangers lurked.

It was important that they concentrate on completing their journey as quickly as possible. The cold was one danger. Crossing ice-covered streams was another. And the presence of desperately hungry animals was still another.

This day was drawing to a close. The brief period of daylight the men had enjoyed was fading away. They were beginning to search for a suitable place to camp for the night, when they heard a dreaded sound. It was a faint cry at first, but it rose on the still air before dying away. It was followed by a second cry, and then a third, each coming from behind them.

Bill and Henry glanced at one another across Lord Alfred's wooden box. Each nodded, aware of what those distant cries meant. A pack of wolves was approaching, and they were after the sled, its dogs, and the men themselves.

Henry broke a long silence, saying what was obvious to both men: "Those wolves want us pretty badly, Bill."

"I know," Bill answered. "They don't have any other meat. I haven't seen a sign of a rabbit in days. I guess they figure that we and our dogs are all they have available."

With that said, they went back to their business. During the remaining hour or so, they listened for further sounds of the wolfpack. Finally they camped among some spruce trees close by a frozen stream. Bill freed the dogs and fed them, while Henry began preparing supper.

They sat down, each on one end of Lord Alfred's coffin. The area between them served as a table. As they ate their beans and drank coffee, they noticed the dogs huddling close to the fire.

Henry laughed. "Those are pretty wise dogs," he said. "They know those wolves are following us. And they know it's not wise to stray very far from camp. I guess you can say that those dogs would rather eat grub than be grub for wolves."

Bill had been eating quietly. "Speaking of grub, Henry," he said, "did you notice how the dogs were acting when I fed them?"

"I could tell they were pretty nervous and noisy. But that isn't surprising, considering how close those wolves are."

Bill was quiet again for several moments. He seemed to be working something out in his mind. At last he asked, "Henry, how many dogs do we have?"

"Six, of course. We started out with six, and we haven't lost any."

"Well then," Bill spoke with hesitation, "if we have six dogs ... can you tell me how I fed them six fish ... and was one fish short?"

"I can tell you all right. You counted wrong."

"No, I didn't. I counted out six fish from the bag, and I gave one to each dog. One Ear didn't get any fish. I had to go back to the bag to get him one."

With a sigh of impatience Henry looked across the fire and counted the dogs.

"There are just six dogs lying there now," he said.

"But one of them ran off after I fed them," Bill replied firmly. "I saw seven."

At that moment, the cries began again. From every direction the men heard them. The dogs, frightened by the sounds, huddled closer to the fire. They were close enough that the heat scorched the hair on a couple of them.

Bill threw some more wood on the fire, lit his pipe, and gazed out into the blackness of the Arctic night. He touched Henry's shoulder and pointed at something on the edge of the blackness. Henry followed Bill's lead and gazed at what looked like two live coals gleaming just above the snow. As he slowly turned his head, he saw a second such pair of coals. And then others came into view. They were the eyes of the wolves, which had made a circle around the camp.

Bill had an urge to pull out his rifle and shoot at those gleaming eyes. Then he remembered that he had only three cartridges left for the rifle. He needed to save these in case the situation grew worse. If only there were three hundred instead of three, Bill was sure he would have blazed away at those threatening eyes.

"So you're thinking one of those wolves came in with the dogs and took one of your fish?" Henry asked.

"That's what I'm thinking," Bill said, "but I don't understand why the dogs would have let a wolf do that."

Neither man had an answer to that question. They turned their attention to preparing their beds. They made sure their campfire was well-supplied with wood for the night and slipped under their blankets. They were soon sound asleep. It did not worry them that the wolves might move into their camp. Like most wild animals, wolves fear fire.

Their sleep was interrupted once when the dogs began making an uproar. Bill got up, fed the fire, and glanced briefly at the dogs. When he was in bed again, he noticed there were seven animals huddled together. But he was too sleepy to let that bother him.

In the morning, even before it was daylight, the men were up, preparing to resume their journey. Henry cooked their breakfast. Bill rolled up their bedding and put the sled in order, so that the dogs could be lashed to it. Then he turned his attention to the dogs.

"Henry!" he shouted, "one of our dogs is missing!"

Henry hurried over to Bill's side. "Which one is missing?" he asked.

Bill knew his dogs, and he was able to answer quickly. "It's Fatty! He's run off and has surely been eaten by the wolves!"

"Why would he leave the camp, when he knew those wolves were out there?"

"I don't have an answer to that, Henry," Bill told him, "but I just remembered something strange. When I got up last night, I thought I

saw seven dogs again. And now we only have five."

The two stood quietly for a moment, eyeing their remaining dogs. They did not have time to discuss these strange happenings. Each soon returned to his chores.

They ate their breakfast in silence. With their five remaining dogs they soon set off on another day's journey. Once again the daylight was with them for only a short while. Once again the Arctic night quickly came upon them. But this day was different in one way: the wolves' cries followed them all day and into the night.

They had made camp, and Henry was finishing the cooking of the beans, when he heard three sounds one right after another. The first was that of a blow being landed. The second was an animal's yelp of pain. And the third was a shout of triumph from Bill.

He stood up to see what was happening. There was a dark shape moving away from the

camp into the blackness. With a look of satisfaction Bill watched it disappear. He was holding a club in one hand and a half-eaten fish
in the other. It was clear that the "seventh
dog" had come in again. Bill had recognized it
as he fed the dogs, and whacked it with the
club.

As they sat on the coffin later, finishing
their meal, they talked about the strange
animal.

"I didn't see it very well," Henry said.
"What kind of animal did you hit with that
club?"

Bill took a last sip of coffee and stared into
the fire. "I wish I could tell you, Henry, but I
didn't get a very good look at it myself. The
best I can say is that it had four legs, a mouth,
and hair, and it looked like a dog."

"Well, it surely isn't any dog!" Henry
exclaimed. "Those wolves out there surely
would have eaten it, if it was. It must be a
tame wolf. That's the only way you can

explain how it knows enough to come into camp to eat."

To their alarm, another dog was missing in the morning! This time it was Frog, the strongest member of their team. Bill decided it was time to tie the dogs up when they camped.

He used the method the Indians practiced. First, he fastened a leather thong around the neck of each dog. Then he tied to this thong a sturdy piece of wood about four to five feet in length. This in turn he tied to a stake in the ground. All of this was arranged so that no dog would be able to reach any of the thongs with his teeth and gnaw through them.

Henry and Bill had not yet gone to their beds when One Ear began whining and whimpering. He lunged toward the darkness, but his leather binding held him back. Without success he chewed at the piece of wood that shielded the leather from him.

The men soon saw the reason for One Ear's excitement. A she-wolf moved softly into the light of the campfire. She remained a cautious distance from the men as she gave most of her attention to the dogs.

Henry now realized what had been happening. He leaned over toward Bill and whispered, "Now, we know what's been happening. That she-wolf is acting as a lure for the wolf pack. She drew Fatty and Frog from the camp. Then the wolves could easily attack. And now, look—she's trying to do the same to One Ear."

Bill nodded, and in a low voice he said, "You're right. I have no doubt that that's the animal I whacked with the club last night. But I still don't understand how a wolf could come right into our camp."

"Maybe if we keep quiet and watch her, we'll find out." Henry glanced toward his rifle. "And maybe we'll stop her before she lures any more dogs away."

The she-wolf did not stay long. A burning log in the campfire fell apart with a loud cracking sound. The startled animal leaped from the camp back into the darkness.

CHAPTER 2

Showdown with a She-Wolf

The morning after their first good look at the she-wolf, Bill made a decision about what he had to do.

"I'm going to get a shot at that wolf," he announced. "We can't afford to lose any more dogs."

"You've only got three cartridges," Henry answered. "We can't afford to lose those either."

"I won't shoot until I have a clear shot at her," Bill assured him.

Bill headed over to where the dogs were awaiting their breakfast. He stopped, counted, looked more closely, then turned back to Henry.

"Spanker's gone," he said.

Henry arose from the fire, where he was cooking the men's breakfast. He counted also, and nodded in agreement.

"But how did he get loose?" Bill was saying. "I had all the dogs tied so they couldn't gnaw through the leather and get away."

"The only thing I can figure," said Henry, "is that One Ear chewed on Spanker's thong. Maybe One Ear decided if he couldn't be free himself, he'd make sure Spanker was free."

They finished their chores, ate breakfast, and resumed their traveling. About one hundred yards into their journey, they found all that was left of Spanker. Bill reached down to pick up something his snowshoe had struck. It was the stick that had been tied to the missing dog.

Bill's determination to shoot the she-wolf was even stronger now. For a while he left Henry to drive the sled and, with rifle in hand, he disappeared into the grayness of mid-afternoon.

About an hour later he caught up with the sled. He took shortcuts in places where the sled had to go around a hill or a cluster of trees. While he was gone he had not fired a shot, but he had seen the wolves. They were very thin, he reported, and other than the three dogs had probably not eaten anything in weeks. In their desperate hunger they posed a serious threat to the two men and their remaining dogs.

Only a few minutes after Bill had rejoined him, Henry saw something on the trail a short distance behind them. When they stopped the sled, the she-wolf came into view. She also stopped but did not run away.

They had their best opportunity yet to examine the creature. She was large for a wolf. Her coat was gray, but it also had a faintly reddish appearance. In her eyes they read the fierce longing for food. To her they were only meat she and her companions were desperate to have.

25

"She's only a short distance from us," Bill whispered. "We may never have a better chance than now to shoot her."

"All right," Henry answered. "Just remember that we can't afford to waste any bullets."

Bill moved slowly, carefully, as he slid the gun from the sled. He held his breath and raised the weapon to his shoulder. The animal was in his sights. He pressed his finger gently against the trigger.

He never had a chance to fire. The she-wolf darted away from the trail and disappeared. She obviously knew what a gun was, just as she had known about the feeding of the dogs. It was becoming obvious that she had been in contact with human beings before.

Bill replaced the gun, disappointed that he had missed this opportunity. But his jaw was set in an unshakable intention.

"I'm going to get her, Henry!" he declared. "She's the cause of all our problems. If she

had not come along, we would have six dogs instead of three. I'm going to watch for her, and you can be sure I'm going to get her!"

That night Henry had difficulty sleeping. It was not fear of the wolves that kept him awake. He was concerned about Bill. On the one hand his partner was growing so determined to kill the she-wolf that he seemed almost reckless. He did not seem concerned about his own safety. On the other hand Bill appeared to be losing hope of their survival. He was beginning to talk like a man who felt helpless against the wolves' pursuit.

The following morning brought a brief change for the better. They still had three dogs, and Bill was in a better mood than during the previous evening. As this day's journey began, Henry was hopeful that their prospects were about to improve.

At midday their outlook turned suddenly worse. First, the sled turned over and was jammed between a rock and the trunk of a tree. Then, when they unharnessed the dogs so they could free the sled, One Ear ran off. As the dog bounded across the snow, they saw that the she-wolf was waiting for him. She immediately began to lure him farther and farther away from the sled.

With the sled in its awkward position Bill was unable to get to the rifle quickly. When he finally pulled it out, One Ear and the she-wolf were too far away and too close together for him to shoot.

One Ear sensed his mistake at this moment and started to return to the sled. As he did, a dozen wolves appeared, coming at him from one direction. Several more came from elsewhere, and the she-wolf was also now on the attack.

Since he no longer had a direct course to the sled, One Ear changed direction and tried to circle around the wolves. They were close behind him, but he was at least able to keep away from their deadly fangs.

Before Henry could stop him, Bill rushed away with rifle in hand.

He was muttering again about killing the she-wolf. Henry realized that Bill was heading for a point where he, One Ear, and the wolf-pack would meet.

Henry's view of that point was cut off by thick underbrush and several spruce trees. Even though he could not see, he could hear what was happening. He heard three shots, the savage snarling of the wolves, One Ear's howl of pain, and then silence.

For a moment he hoped that he might see Bill returning. It was a vain hope. He finally faced the fact that his friend was dead. Perhaps he had killed three of the wolves with the shots Henry heard. Then the pack must have charged him.

For a long time afterward Henry sat upon the sled. The two surviving dogs huddled near his feet. The wolves had picked off four dogs, and now they had also finished Bill. Henry was saddened, frightened, weary, but he was not about to give up hope. The wolves would not easily have him.

Joining the dogs in pulling the sled with the heavy coffin on it, he traveled only a short distance. He made certain that he had an ample supply of firewood for the night. Trying to keep as calm as possible, he ate his supper and crawled into his bed.

This would not be a night for sleep, however. The wolves moved in closer than ever, apparently aware that he no longer had a way to defend himself. That meant that he had to stay awake and feed the fire, so that it was continuously blazing. And when the wolves edged too close, he had to pull out flaming brands and hurl them at the animals to drive them back.

To keep his mind occupied he worked out a plan. When the sleepless night was over and the wolves departed at the coming of daylight, he put the plan into action. Chopping down some nearby saplings, he tied them together and formed a kind of scaffold or platform. He tied this to the trunks of two tall trees, so that it hung between them several feet above the ground.

Now came the most difficult part of his plan. Fastening one end of a rope to the coffin, he curled the other end around a high limb on one of the trees. Then, catching that loose end as it slid down from the limb, he tugged with all his strength. He was at last able to hoist the coffin onto the platform. The wolves had taken Bill. They might soon also take him. But Henry made certain they would never get to the lifeless body of Lord Alfred.

With that task done, he harnessed the dogs to the lightened sled and headed for Fort McGurry. His only hope lay in reaching the fort before the wolves were able to make one more attack.

He did not dare travel after dark. Even before daylight completely faded, he made camp and chopped as much firewood as he could. Then he built his fire and crouched down by it. With the dogs trembling and whimpering beside him, he settled down for another night.

In spite of his danger he fell asleep briefly on several occasions. Each time he would awaken to find one of the wolves only a few feet away, staring hungrily at him. The fire was still burning brightly enough to keep the beasts from lunging in upon him.

The lack of sleep began to affect his thinking. At one point he idly held out his hand and moved his fingers. He was fascinated at the marvelous way his body worked. He had never thought about this before. Skin, muscles, bones, nerves, the organs inside his body— what an amazing being he was! And yet, for those few dozen wolves that had made a circle around him, he was no more than meat. He was only a meal they were eager to enjoy.

When morning came, the wolves did not scatter as they had before. He made an effort to pull out on the trail, but was forced back to the fire when the boldest of them leaped and barely missed him. Then he hurled brands from the fire in every direction to drive the pack away.

He had to use his wits to keep up his supply of firewood. A little ways from his campfire was a large dead spruce. To get to it, he spent a few hours gradually moving his fire toward the tree. When he reached it, he made sure to fell it so that the tree lay near other dead trees.

Another terrible night followed. Again he fought to stay awake. Again he slipped into brief periods of sleep. Once when he awoke, the she-wolf stood within a yard of him. He drove her off for a while by thrusting a brand into her mouth. Before he fell asleep again, he tied a burning pine knot to his right hand. Several times he did this, so that he was awakened by the flame as it burned his flesh.

Finally he tied the pine knot so poorly that it fell off. He slept. He dreamed a dream of wolves attacking him. He awoke to find the dream was real. The wolves were indeed upon him. Only by desperately hurling the live coals was he able to drive them off.

When he was again standing alone beside the protecting light of the fire, he noticed that the remaining two dogs were missing. The wolves had now finished off the entire team. And of course Bill was also gone.

But I am still alive, he said to himself, *and I intend to fight to the end.*

"You don't have me yet!" he shouted. He shook his fist in rage at the beasts. They snarled in response and continued to focus their hungry gaze upon him.

He tried one more idea. Spreading out the flaming brands he built a circle of flame and huddled down inside of it. The wolves made

their own circle outside of it, and they began a terrible howling that lasted through the rest of the night.

Daylight came, and Henry saw that places within his circle were dying out. He found that the wolves would not let him reach any more wood. The end had come, it seemed. He crouched back down in the center of the circle and watched the flames sputter and go out in various spots. If he was about to die, he decided, then he might as well go to sleep.

And so he slept. He awakened once, saw a large opening in the circle, and watched the she-wolf sliding through it. The last thing he remembered before falling asleep again was that dreadful look of hunger in her eyes.

When he awoke the next time, he was surprised to find that he was still alive. Furthermore, he noted that his body was free of the pain that wolf bites would have caused. Through heavy eyelids he saw that the wolves were gone. He tried to organize his thoughts and struggled to understand how he had been spared.

And then he heard the sounds of men approaching with dogs and sleds. The wolves had obviously heard those sounds earlier, and they had been frightened away. He was safe, but when his rescuers reached him, he could not express any relief or rejoicing.

"What have you done with Lord Alfred's body?" one man asked him.

"It's back there," he answered, pointing a wobbly finger toward the trail. "I hung his coffin from a tree limb."

Another man shook him as his eyelids closed. "You don't have any dogs for your sled. Where are they?"

With his last bit of strength Henry replied angrily, "The wolves ate them. They ate all six of them. And they ate Bill, too. Didn't you see the wolves?"

The man shook his head. "If there were any wolves around here, they are gone now."

Before that sentence was finished, Henry had fallen into a deep sleep.

CHAPTER 3

A Mate and a Lair

Wolves run in packs when it is to their advantage to do so. When they are trying to kill a large animal for its meat, it is obviously helpful to have a few dozen attackers coming at the beast from all directions. Two or three wolves might be driven off by flying hooves or thrusting antlers. But a whole pack of wolves will sooner or later wear down the largest victim.

When game is plentiful, the wolves no longer need to be in packs. A male and female wolf by themselves can catch enough rabbits, squirrels, and other smaller animals to satisfy their appetites.

The wolfpack that nearly killed Henry remained together for a while after being frightened away by the men who came to Henry's rescue. On the day following that incident, the starving wolves finally found meat to quiet their desperate hunger.

They sighted moose grazing in a low plain, and in particular they set their attention on a big bull moose that weighed more than eight hundred pounds. Its size and the dangers posed by its mighty hooves and sharp antlers did not cause them to hesitate.

They were a deadly pack. Though some of them were broken and bleeding by the time it was done, they brought down the giant beast.

The moose supplied meat for about forty wolves. Each member of the pack filled his or her stomach with some twenty pounds of food. And that was just the beginning. In the days that followed they feasted upon more moose and other game.

Soon the pack started breaking up. First, it split in half. The she-wolf went with a smaller pack, which was led by an old one-eyed male wolf. That pack also broke up, with pairs of wolves, male and female, gradually going their separate ways. At last the she-wolf had only three companions. One was the one-eyed leader. There were also a younger leader and a three-year-old male.

The three males were all determined to have the she-wolf as a mate. With this aim in mind they promptly forgot about how they had endured near-starvation together. Now they directed their fangs toward one another.

Their battle began when the three-year-old attacked the one-eyed wolf on his blind side. He succeeded in ripping the older beast's ear, but he quickly lost the advantage of his surprise. The older wolf had experience from many past battles. This enabled him to respond by slashing his foe's side.

The two were evenly matched, and either might have won, had it remained one against one. But the third male suddenly joined the fight, taking on the three-year-old. With two against one, the contest was quickly decided. The three-year-old lay dead in the snow.

To a human observer, the one-eyed wolf should have been grateful for his younger companion's assistance.

But this was still war, a war fought according to something other than human rules. When the younger rival turned his head to lick a wound, One Eye sank his teeth into his rival's throat and burst a blood vessel. In a few minutes this younger leader was also dead.

The she-wolf watched all this with a kind of quiet satisfaction. Earlier, when the three males had touched her, she had responded with snarls and the snapping of her teeth. But now her mate was decided. She greeted him with friendly sniffing. Then she playfully leaped about with him. The two behaved like young puppies, forgetting their ages and the brutal fights they had endured. They followed this with a vigorous chase through the woods.

Soon they settled down to a life together as partners. Side by side they hunted, killed game, and ate it. They traveled along the Mackenzie River, where they often met other wolves. They ignored those that were paired as they were. But when they encountered a male that showed an interest in joining them, they stood together, fangs bared, until the stranger left them.

During this time the she-wolf began searching. She looked into caves, hollows, and other openings in the earth for a place to bear the cubs that were growing inside of her. One Eye patiently waited as she searched for just the right place to give birth.

Near the river one night they came upon an Indian camp. The sounds, sights, and smells were all strange to One Eye. He was suspicious and fearful, and he wanted to go on. But the she-wolf was drawn to this strange scene, for it was something she had known before. She felt an urge to go in to the campfire, to be near the Indians and their dogs.

A stronger urge pulled her away. She had to find that place she was searching for. Nature impressed upon her the duty of bearing her young and nursing them. And so, to One Eye's relief, she joined him in slipping away from the camp, back into the forest.

As they moved among the spruce trees, One Eye spied a flash of white ahead. It was a snowshoe rabbit and he bounded after it. But this rabbit was not running. Instead, it was dancing in the air, high above the ground. One Eye leaped up and sank his teeth into the white body.

As he came back to earth he was startled by a cracking sound. Then he saw a sapling bending over and coming at him. In fright he released the rabbit, and it soared high into the air again.

The she-wolf understood what One Eye did not. The rabbit was caught in a snare made by men. It was the snare that had caught the rabbit's foot and lifted the creature into the air. Held high by the sapling connected to the snare, the rabbit struggled and wriggled and appeared to be dancing.

But she did not show any sympathy for her mate over his puzzled reaction to this human device. In anger she set upon him for his failure. He struck back only briefly and then struggled to protect himself.

When she was done, she sat down in the snow and waited. Fearing his mate more than this mysterious sapling, he sprang up again and caught the rabbit. Once again the tree bent toward him, but this time he did not release his prize. For a moment he remained in place, holding onto the rabbit and growling at the sapling hovering above him. Then the she-wolf stepped in and chewed off the rabbit's head. The sapling shot back up into its

normal position, and the two of them enjoyed their hard-earned meal.

In this way the she-wolf taught One Eye the skill of robbing human snares. In days to come that would prove to be a valuable lesson.

The time arrived when hunting food was less important to the she-wolf than finding a place of shelter. Like all female animals she knew somehow that she was responsible for giving birth and caring for her young ones. She knew she needed a home.

Wolves' homes are called lairs. What the she-wolf was searching for was a lair, and her need was becoming urgent. The cubs forming within her were having an effect on her. As she grew heavier, she was not able to run so swiftly as before. She also required more rest after running, and as One Eye discovered, her anger erupted now more quickly than ever.

The need was finally supplied. The two were traveling along a frozen stream that flowed in summertime into the Mackenzie. The she-wolf spied a cave in the clay bank above the ice-covered streambed. It had been made by spring rains and melting snow, which washed away a portion of the bank.

She examined the outside of the cave carefully. Then she squeezed her body into its narrow entrance. Once inside she found herself in a snug area about six feet long and wide. Her decision was made: this was the place she had been looking for. With a look of contentment she lay down, her head pointed toward the entrance where One Eye stood.

When he saw that his mate intended to stay, One Eye went out alone to hunt. He had no success. The melting snow made his footing more difficult. He chased a few snowshoe rabbits, but their wide paws, for which they are named, enabled them to escape across the snow. The wolf broke through the soft crust.

One Eye returned to the lair and realized immediately that something was different. He heard strange whimpering sounds coming from within, and he knew his mate was not making them. Crouching down to enter the cave he saw five tiny, squirming things lying against the she-wolf's body. They were making the noises he had heard.

He was surprised, even though in his long life he had fathered cubs before. He was also curious, but he learned quickly that he dared not move any closer. The she-wolf growled and snarled at him when he made any movement toward her. She knew, as every wolf mother knows by nature, that male wolves sometimes kill and eat the cubs they father.

Once again One Eye left the lair to hunt. Only this time his hunting served a different purpose. Nature was also guiding him. If his mate was to have food during this important time in her life, he would have to provide it.

This time he would enjoy success. But it would come in an unusual way. When he came upon a porcupine gnawing upon the bark of a tree, he approached it carefully. He had never eaten one of these animals and knew they were not easy to catch. The sharp quills on their back and tail gave them great protection. One Eye had once carried one of those painful needles in his muzzle for weeks. He did not want to suffer that again.

Catching sight of him the porcupine rolled into a ball. Its quills stuck out in every direction. The wolf waited for about half an hour, hoping for an opportunity to thrust his teeth beneath those quills. When the porcupine remained in the same position, he gave up his wait and went in search of some easier prey.

He had better luck a little later. By chance he came face-to-face with a ptarmigan. Having caught and killed the bird, he started to eat it. Then he remembered his mate's needs.

Picking up the ptarmigan in his mouth, he turned back in the direction of the lair.

His trail took him past the place where he had seen the porcupine. As he neared that spot, he saw some large tracks in the snow. He knew that he did not want to meet the maker of those tracks head-on. Therefore, he moved cautiously along the stream that led back to the lair.

Coming around a large rock, he saw the porcupine, rolled again in its quill-covered ball. One Eye crouched down and watched. Low against the snow, waiting for the quills to lower, was a female lynx. It was she who had made the tracks. She was the one the wolf wanted to avoid.

Hidden by the needles of a spruce he looked on for more than an hour as the lynx silently waited. At last there was movement. The porcupine apparently believed the danger was past. He was unaware of the lynx's presence, so he began to stretch out and to lower his quills.

In a flash the lynx struck out with one paw. Her claws ripped across the underside of the porcupine, opening up a deadly wound. But the wounded animal also struck. His barbed tail came down on the lynx's paw. The cat wailed in agony for a moment. Then in anger she attacked the porcupine again. All she got for this effort was a nose full of quills as her victim caught her again with his prickly tail.

One Eye saw that his opportunity had come. The lynx was wildly running away, trying in vain to find some way of freeing her nose from the painful barbs. The once untouchable porcupine was dying. The wolf waited until the badly bleeding creature lay still. Then he ate the ptarmigan and dragged the porcupine to the lair.

The she-wolf seemed grateful for the food. But she still made it clear that she would not let him come near the tiny cubs she was nursing.

Had One Eye been able to examine his cubs, he would have discovered that one of them looked like him. This male cub was gray and differed from his father only in that he had two eyes to his father's one. Like most newborns in the animal world he spent the earliest days of his life eating and sleeping. His world was his mother's body, providing food and warmth and security.

It was not long before he was ready to explore the lair and learn more about it. Some of his first lessons had to do with the wall of light he saw at the cave's entrance. He learned that his father could walk through that wall, bringing meat for his mate. Then he could walk back through it and disappear.

The wall of light also taught him what pain was. Along with his two brothers and two sisters he was drawn to that light. When he would yield to the attraction of the light and crawl toward it, his mother would strike him with her paw and move him back into the lair.

His next learning experience was how to avoid pain. He became aware of just how close he could get to the light before his mother struck. Thus, he was able to stop just short of that point. And even when he passed that point, he began to develop the skill of dodging and avoiding the punishing paw.

In his play with the other cubs he soon learned to use his own paw effectively. He could, with a swift stroke, cause one of his brothers or sisters to go tumbling over. His teeth, he found, were useful for gripping the ears of his fellow cubs. He also developed the beginning of a growl.

But one of his most difficult lessons to learn was that of hunger. His first food was, of course, his mother's milk. But that soon dried up. Even before it did, the she-wolf began to feed her cubs meat. She took some of the game One Eye brought, chewed it, partly digested it, and then coughed it up again in a form the cubs could eat.

61

The time came, however, when One Eye's hunting gained nothing. He was no longer able to rob the rabbit snares, since the Indians moved their camp away. The she-wolf left her litter several times to join the hunting, but she too was unsuccessful.

One by one the cubs grew weaker and died. At last only the gray cub survived, and he also came close to death. But he was the strongest of the litter. He lived on and continued to be drawn to that strange wall of light.

His father no longer came through that wall. The gray cub did not know why, but the she-wolf did. On one of her searches for food she found his remains on the trail. It was clear that One Eye had finally met the lynx in battle, and the lynx had come away the winner.

CHAPTER 4

Through the Wall of Light

Curiosity is a characteristic of both human beings and animals. Out of a sense of curiosity we probe the vastness of space, the depths of the oceans, and the mysteries of the tiniest forms of life.

Animals do not share our power of reason. They do not develop formulas or write books or invent machines. But they are also curious about their world and drawn to explore it.

On one of those occasions when his mother was out hunting, the gray cub felt curiosity powerfully drawing him. At last he dared to go through the wall of light.

65

Fear had kept him from doing this earlier. He had learned fear when his mother struck him during his earlier approaches toward that wall. He had another fearful experience when he explored the back wall of the lair and smashed his muzzle painfully against the packed earth. Then there was the day he had crouched in fear inside the lair, sensing that something dangerous lurked just beyond the wall. A wolverine was indeed investigating the entrance to the cave. Because it heard nothing inside, it went on its way.

The day came when the urge to explore became greater than his fear. Since his mother and her threatening paw were away, there was nothing to keep him from heading for the wall. He found that it was not hard as the back wall had been. Instead, it seemed to give way as he pressed on into it.

When he reached the opening of the cave, he was almost blinded by the light. As his eyes adjusted, he looked out on a world of things he had never seen before. There were trees, the glistening stream, the distant top of a mountain, and above him the pale blue sky.

He stood on the edge of a slope above the stream, but he did not know what a slope was. Up to this time, his world had been a level one. Now when he stepped forward, he suddenly found himself tumbling down, down, down, until he came to a halt on a level, grassy area.

His fear had turned briefly to terror during the fall. But curiosity was growing stronger. The desire to explore and learn made him forget to be afraid of the unknown. He saw the first living creature other than a wolf that he had ever seen. It was a squirrel playing around the dead trunk of a pine tree. The two spied each other at the same moment, and each was frightened. But the wolf cub's fear quickly gave way to his interest in this world of new things and experiences.

His next discovery was birds. First came a woodpecker. It startled him with its flapping of wings when it soared into the air, but again he promptly forgot that. Next he came across a moose-bird. This creature was bold enough to hop right up to him. The cub reached out a paw, not in a threatening way, but as a playful gesture. The bird reacted with alarm, pecking the cub on the nose and fluttering away.

In spite of these experiences his confidence and courage grew. He scrambled up on top of a fallen pine trunk and stepped along its length. But he lost his footing and took another tumble. This time he ended up right in the middle of a nest of ptarmigan chicks.

He regarded them playfully at first. Then he became aware of how hungry he was. Picking up one of the chicks in his mouth, he crunched down with his teeth. It was the beginning of a meal that would not end until all seven chicks were gone.

He was about to find that the meal came at a troublesome price. As he left the now-empty

nest, the angry mother ptarmigan appeared. Her wildly flapping wings caught him off guard, and he covered his head with his paws to protect himself from her attack.

After a few moments of enduring the striking of the wings, he was also angry. He caught one of the wings in his teeth and held on stubbornly. Not only was he protecting himself— he was fighting for food. The chicks had not fully satisfied his hunger. This larger creature was also meat that he was determined to have.

The ptarmigan struggled to free herself as she continued to flap her free wing against him. But for several minutes he refused to let go. At last the two of them lay quietly, exhausted by the battle. Then she began to peck him on his already-sore nose. Tiring of this he released her and ran over to the shade of some nearby bushes.

The cub was not to have the ptarmigan for meat, but another hungry creature would.

While the cub watched, a hawk darted down out of the sky, sank its claws into the surprised bird, and carried it away out of sight.

In all this the cub was learning lessons of life and survival. He was beginning to understand a basic rule of the Wild: there were creatures you could eat, and there were creatures that could eat you. He was aware that the hawk could have swooped down on him as easily as on the ptarmigan.

He seemed to be moving from one fearful experience to another. His third fall of this eventful day sent him splashing into the stream. His head plunged beneath the water, and he was unable to breathe. But he popped back to the surface and, with Nature's guidance, actually began to swim.

Before he could reach the shore, the current picked him up. His body was carried swiftly downstream. It bumped against one rock after another until he finally tumbled into a small, quiet pool of water. He regained his

footing on a bed of gravel and climbed up on the bank away from the stream.

By this time he had enough of exploring. He remembered the lair and his mother, and he was anxious to find her again. Tired and sleepy, he wanted to lie down in the cave.

One more painful encounter with the world awaited him. When he met a young weasel, who was also out exploring, he was not afraid of it. He cornered it, reached out with his paw, and turned it over. But like the mother ptarmigan, the mother weasel was not far away. Appearing suddenly, she struck a swift blow to the cub's neck with her teeth. Then she picked up her young one and dashed away with it.

The cub was whimpering over the pain in his neck and longing for the safety of the lair when the mother weasel returned. Her young one was now safe. She was prepared to fight with this intruder and finish him off. When she launched her attack, she fastened her teeth on the neck of the cub. She intended to break into the blood vessel there and feast on the young wolf's blood, which is what weasels seek for their food.

She was close to succeeding in this. The frightened cub did not know how to break her grip. If the weasel had enjoyed only a few more minutes to press in upon his neck, she would have killed him. But the she-wolf arrived in time to save her cub. The weasel released her grip on the cub's neck and turned her attack on the older wolf. But the she-wolf quickly killed her. Then she and her cub ate the weasel before returning to the lair.

The cub needed a couple of days' rest. Then again he was out exploring and now hunting. His only victim was the young weasel, when he came across it again. He saw ptarmigans, but he was unable to catch one. He tried to sneak up on the squirrel outside the cave, but it was always scurrying up a tree before he could sink his teeth into it.

He was not alone in his inability to get meat. His mother, whom he knew was a good hunter, was also unsuccessful. Another period of severe hunger set in. The cub became so desperate for food that he even tried to lure the hawk down, so that he could catch and eat it. He sat out in an open place and waited to challenge the hawk's claws with his young fangs. The bird was too clever to swoop down at that time.

His mother at last brought home meat, unusual meat. She was desperate enough that she raided the lynx's lair. After eating most of the litter herself, she carried the last one home to her cub. He ate it happily and then lay down to sleep.

When he awoke, it was to the sound of his mother's snarling. He looked at the entrance of the cave and saw the lynx mother crouching there. Her own lair had been invaded, and she had come to punish the offender.

The cub could only look on as the two mothers began a fight to the death. The lynx had a slight advantage in that she had both claws and teeth as weapons, while the she-wolf was armed only with her teeth.

As the battle raged, he tried to help. On two occasions he sank his teeth into a hind leg of the lynx. For his efforts he was nearly crushed when the two rolled on top of him. And he suffered the most severe pain he had ever known when the cat's claws ripped open his shoulder. But he showed courage, helping

his mother until the battle ended with the death of the lynx.

The fight had taken so much out of the she-wolf that she needed several days to rest and heal. With his shoulder torn and bleeding, the cub also required time to recover. It was a full week before they ate the body of the defeated lynx.

The lesson he had begun to learn earlier was becoming clearer. Life in the Wild was a matter of "Eat, or be eaten." More and more he lived by that law, as he joined his mother in hunting. More and more he gained not only food, but pleasure and excitement in chasing and capturing game.

CHAPTER 5

Captured!

In some way animals recognize man's superior intelligence and are awed by that. To them man possesses a kind of majesty. At least, that was how man seemed to the wolf cub on the day that he first encountered man. It was a day that would change the course of his life.

It was quite by accident that the cub first came into the presence of man. On that morning he left the cave and went down to the stream to drink. When he trotted into a nearby cluster of trees, he saw them. There were five of them, and they were squatting down, talking with one another. When they saw him, they showed no fear, nor were they quick to move toward him. They merely sat and watched him, without making a sound.

He could easily have run back to the lair, but something made him stay. Perhaps it was the power these creatures seemed to possess. Perhaps Nature herself drew him to these impressive beings. Whatever it was, he not only stayed. He actually lowered himself to the ground, as though he were submitting to them.

The men were Indians, and they began to speak in their language about the cub. One of them walked over to him as he crouched on the ground. When the man reached over as if to touch him, he began to growl slightly, and he bared his fangs. Instead of backing away, the man laughed and called to his companions, "Look! He has white fangs!"

As the other men joined in the laughter, the one who stood over the cub reached down again. When the hand was almost touching him, the cub forgot his awe and sank his teeth into it. But in the next moment he found himself lying on his side. His head was ringing from a blow the man delivered with his other hand. The cub sat up and made a little wailing sound, and the man reacted by landing a second blow to his head.

His cry accomplished something. He first heard the snarling. Then he saw the dark form of his mother as she ran in among the trees to rescue him. The men promptly retreated as she examined her cub to make sure he was all right. She turned toward the men, fixing her angry eyes on them and snarling viciously.

The cub was amazed at what happened next. One of the men cried out a single word: "Kiche!" At once his mother changed. The snarling ceased, and her anger vanished. When the man again called, "Kiche!" she crouched down and began whimpering and wagging her tail. He walked over to her and touched her head, and she did not snap at him or begin snarling again.

The Indians were speaking excitedly to one another. They knew this she-wolf. She and her mother had lived with them, and she had been given the name Kiche. She had run away from their camp a year ago.

Gray Beaver, whose brother had owned Kiche and her mother, was now ready to lay claim to the she-wolf and her cub. His brother was dead, he pointed out, so what belonged to his brother now belonged to him.

As if to seal his claim he laid his hand on the cub. When the young wolf snarled, the Indian drew back his hand as if to strike. Having already taken two firm blows from a human hand, the cub became silent and covered his fangs. Gray Beaver instead rubbed him behind the ears and along his back. As he did, he announced to his companions:

"His mother is Kiche,—half dog, half wolf. His father must have been a wolf. He is only one-fourth dog, but he is mine. And because his fangs are white, I will call him White Fang."

Gray Beaver tied Kiche to a tree, and the newly named cub lay down beside her. One of the other Indians had decided to play with the cub. As he was rolled on his back and the man rubbed him on his stomach, White Fang experienced a strange mixture of feelings. Then, after being turned back on his side, he felt the man stroking him behind his ears. Though still fearful of these powerful beings, he experienced a kind of pleasure he had never known before.

Soon the five men were joined by the rest of their tribe. This was a throng made up of more than forty men, women, and children. With them they brought their dogs. When the dogs became aware of the presence of the she-wolf and her cub, they rushed at them with their sharp teeth bared. But the men, using stones and clubs, drove the dogs back.

White Fang had never seen dogs before. Now that he had met them, he quickly learned to dislike them. His hatred for them would soon grow beyond anything he could have imagined. And their feelings toward him would become equally harsh.

On this occasion he had little time to consider the dogs. He was instead amazed even more by the abilities of men. They had exercised an awesome power over the dogs by using dead things like stones and sticks. It was a masterful control they held over the things of the world.

The Indians did not remain long in this place, but resumed their traveling. Kiche was led along the trail by a leash of rawhide attached to a stick. White Fang followed as the tribe made its way along the stream, which led at last to the Mackenzie River. The Indians made their camp by the river.

White Fang was awed by the tepees that soon arose by the river's edge. The tall poles covered by cloth and animal skins towered above him. As he looked at the tops reaching into the sky, he crouched in fear.

As had happened on the first day that he ventured out of the cave, he now found his fear giving way to the urge to explore. He touched one of the tepees and sniffed at it. He even fastened his teeth to an end of it and tugged. A squaw inside cried out when the tepee began swaying, and White Fang hurried back to where Kiche was.

For a while he forgot about the dogs. He was about to learn that his earlier experience with them was an indication of what life would be like with the dogs in the camp. On this first day he met the dog that would be his chief problem and with which he would share the strongest hatred.

This dog's name was Lip-lip. He was actually only a puppy, but an older and larger puppy than White Fang. When they met for the first time, White Fang was ready to be friendly. Lip-lip's low growl and the stiffness of his walk showed he was not interested in friendship.

Seeing that he was going to have to fight, White Fang snarled at the dog and began to move toward him. Lip-lip responded with a quick leap and a snap, and White Fang felt sharp teeth in his shoulder. In the next few moments he would feel those teeth in his ear, his leg, and his side.

White Fang fought with courage, but Lip-lip enjoyed a size advantage and the experience of many earlier fights in the camp. He was an easy winner in this first battle between the two.

White Fang's terrible encounter with Lip-lip sent him scurrying back to his mother's side. But curiosity soon overcame fear once again. He watched Gray Beaver spreading sticks and dry moss on the ground. Some of the women and children were bringing more sticks and building a pile of them in front of the man.

As White Fang looked on, smoke began to curl ot from the pile. And then, a dancing yellow flame appeared above the sticks. He had never seen either smoke or fire, and he pressed in more closely to it.

It is a normal practice for any animal to sniff at something new and strange to it. And that was what White Fang did. At the same time he extended his tongue toward it. Searing pain sent him scrambling and yelping back to his mother. His nose and tongue would be sore the rest of the day.

His body would heal from the savage touch of the flame. But something else happened that would have a much more enduring effect on him. Gray Beaver laughed at him in his hurt and confusion, and the other Indians joined in the laughter. Though he was an animal, he felt a kind of embarrassment. And from the beginning, he resented the sound of human laughter directed at him.

CHAPTER 6

The Loss
of a Mother

The day comes for any creature when he must separate from his father and mother and live on his own. Among human beings a special tie remains between parents and children long after the children have left home. The parents continue to hold a special affection for their children, and the children maintain a sense of respect and gratitude toward their parents.

Among many animals this is not so. With the kinds of lives they must lead, it is better that the parents and children forget about one another. That was a lesson White Fang would learn, but it would take a long and anxious time to learn it.

Each succeeding day found White Fang exploring and investigating. He continued to grow in his appreciation for what men could do and how they controlled so much of their world. Always, when frightened or hurt, he would return to his mother. It could not occur to him that someday soon they would be separated.

As a newborn cub, he had learned how to avoid the pain of his mother's swiping paw, keeping him away from the wall of light. And now he began to learn fresh lessons of how to keep himself from painful, threatening experiences.

One such lesson came on those occasions when the Indians threw meat or fish to the dogs. He found it was safer to let the older dogs have it. From his earliest days in the camp he understood that he should steer clear of mother dogs with small puppies. Also, he learned that as far as humans were concerned, it was best to stay in the company of the men and women. Children tended to be thoughtless and cruel, and it was best to avoid them.

There was one creature he seemed unable to avoid. Lip-lip took a special delight in attacking him and outfighting him. It seemed that any time White Fang strayed very far from his mother, Lip-lip would appear and deal out a fresh supply of pain and grief.

White Fang could have let fear rule him, but he did not. Instead, he developed his own mean temper. Some of the puppies in the camp would have accepted him as one of their own. He could have romped and played with them. But he stayed away from them all. When he had the chance, he dealt out his own kind of pain on those who were as young and as small as he.

Another way he overcame the fearful aspects of life in the camp was through his cleverness. He used that to find ways of stealing food. He would sneak around the tepees, watching for opportunities. When those opportunities came, he would move with quickness. In this way he was able to get food that the dogs his age could never have had.

One day he put his cleverness to a very special use. He knew *he* could not defeat Lip-lip in a fight. But if that bully ever came face-to-face with Kiche, it would be a different matter. Although White Fang did not know it, Kiche had once lured dogs out of men's camps to provide food for her pack. Now her son was ready to lure a dog into an encounter with her fangs.

White Fang wandered out into the camp and caught Lip-lip's attention, as he had many times before. And, as he also had done previously, he ran from the bigger dog. However, he did not run as swiftly as he could have. It was not his desire to escape from his enemy, but to keep him close behind.

Around and around the tepees they went. Little by little they drew closer to the trap White Fang was setting. In his excitement Lip-

lip failed to see what was about to happen. As they sped around one last tepee, the bully ran almost head-on into Kiche.

Even though she was tied, the she-wolf was able to knock Lip-lip down and slash at him. He frantically struggled to get away, but she would not let him regain his footing. For almost a full minute she continued tearing at his small body.

White Fang took full advantage of the situation. When Lip-lip rolled free of his mother's fangs, the cub rushed in to sink his teeth savagely into the dog's hind leg. The wailing creature ran off, with White Fang at his heels. He only backed away when some squaws pelted him with stones.

Soon afterward he had his mother's protection all of the time. Gray Beaver released Kiche from her tether knowing she would not run away. Now White Fang could walk about the camp by his mother's side, and Lip-lip did not dare come near.

That day of Kiche's release brought an opportunity to escape the camp. White Fang led her out into the woods at the edge of the camp. If he could have convinced her, he would have led her away to search for the lair and its nearby stream. But the hold that the humans had on her was too strong. When she returned to the camp, he reluctantly followed her.

Not long afterward the unthinkable happened: His mother was taken away from him. Gray Beaver owed a debt to another Indian named Three Eagles. He paid part of the debt by giving Kiche to Three Eagles. On that same day Three Eagles prepared to take a lengthy trip up the Mackenzie. He took Kiche into his canoe with the rest of his possessions.

White Fang was desperate to follow. When he tried to climb in the canoe, Three Eagles knocked him away. He recovered to see the canoe moving away from the shore and into the middle of the river. He fearlessly plunged into the waters and began to swim after it.

Gray Beaver cried out his name, but he refused to hear. Staying close to his mother was his only thought. Angrily, Gray Beaver launched his own canoe. Reaching White Fang, he pulled him up out of the water. Then, as he held the cub with one hand, he beat him soundly with the other.

Before they reached shore, White Fang was battered and broken in spirit. During the beating he dared to snarl at Gray Beaver, which made the angry Indian strike even harder. Gray Beaver threw him into the bottom of the boat, and kicked him. White Fang responded by biting the Indian on the foot. This bite brought on a second, more severe beating.

This second beating taught White Fang a painful lesson he would never forget: To bite his human master was the most terrible wrong he could commit. He would not do such a foolish thing again.

The boat reached the shore, and as White Fang whimpered, Gray Beaver threw his small, sore body onto the hard ground. Lip-lip was waiting, and he came rushing with his mouth opened to bare his punishing teeth. The bully made one brief attack, but a powerful kick from Gray Beaver drove him away.

The bitter night that followed brought one more beating. His wailing over the loss of his mother awakened Gray Beaver. One more time the Indian showed his power over the cub, striking him until he became silent.

His grieving for his mother continued for many days, even though he expressed it in a quieter way. In his animal mind he held on to a desperate hope that she would return some-day to him.

In spite of his mother's being taken away, and in spite of the beatings he received, he still respected men and Gray Beaver in particular. He appreciated the pieces of meat Gray Beaver tossed him occasionally. He even developed a kind of attachment to the man, but there was nothing close to affection between them.

One thing did not change. White Fang felt a constant yearning for the life of freedom he had once known. Indeed, there were several times when he would have run away from the camp, had he not hoped his mother would return.

CHAPTER 7

The Return
of a Runaway

Ever since his capture by the Indians, White Fang had longed for the freedom he had known as a young cub. But he also would discover that such a freedom did not satisfy in the way he expected.

Life in the camp had been difficult before. But now, with Kiche's absence, it became brutal. Lip-lip renewed his attacks, and many other dogs followed his lead. White Fang grew even more vicious and also more clever, a quality associated with his nature as a wolf.

He became unpopular with the squaws by robbing meat whenever he could. At the mere sight of him, they would pick up the nearest object and hurl it at him. But he was alert and able to dodge the items thrown and move to a place of safety.

As for his fights with the dogs, he would have won in most of these, had they been a matter of one-on-one combat. But he seldom enjoyed that situation. Usually he had to battle an entire pack at one time. Even in these fights he did well. He was always able to keep them from knocking him off his feet. This was vital, because an animal on its back or side had its throat exposed to attack.

He used this knowledge effectively on those occasions when he caught a dog alone. With a surprise attack he quickly knocked his victim off its feet and sank his young fangs into its throat. At this point in his life he was not strong enough to kill a foe in this way, but he could still do a great deal of damage.

When he did not want to fight, he knew how to scare off an opponent. He used his snarl, which developed into the most terrible and threatening snarl of any animal in the camp. Even the older and larger dogs would hesitate to attack him when he began his vicious snarling.

As time passed, he used his snarl less and his fangs more. His jaws at last became powerful enough for him to drive into an opponent's throat and rip open a blood vessel. When he began killing puppies in this way, their owners were prompt in complaining to Gray Beaver. But White Fang's master refused to heed their complaints. He knew that the other dogs took every opportunity they found to trouble White Fang. If White Fang took revenge on one of them, the Indian felt it was only right.

It seemed that Gray Beaver was his only friend. He was hated by almost all of the other Indians. Of course, the dogs only attacked him when they had the numbers to do so. Even Gray Beaver was not really a friend, but merely a master. He offered no kindness or affection to White Fang, and the wolf gave none in return. The one factor that kept White Fang at the camp was his continuing hope that his mother would come back.

The day came when he made his decision to leave the Indians. It came on a frosty day in the fall when the tribe took down their tepees and loaded their belongings into canoes. They were preparing to do their fall hunting downstream.

It was easy for him, in the midst of all the activity, to slip out of the camp into the woods. He had chosen this time to run away, and he knew he would need to hide his trail. To do this he tramped for a time in an icy, but still running, stream. Finally, in the cover provided by some thick bushes, he rested and slept.

He awoke once to hear Gray Beaver calling him. There were other voices: Kloo-kooch, Gray Beaver's squaw, and Mit-sah, his son.

White Fang remained still and resisted a strange urge to respond to the voice of his master. At last he heard the voices no longer, and he knew he was free.

Despite his freedom, it did not take long before he began to yearn for the camp. In the place where he lay no fire blazed to drive back the darkness and provide warmth. His feet became especially cold, and he found no way to protect them. The darkness disturbed him, for he feared it might conceal some danger about to fall upon him.

Soon he became hungry. In the camp he had depended on the humans for food. Now he would have to hunt again, and there might be nothing to hunt. He remembered and hungered for the meat and fish the Indians had thrown to him, and he wanted to return to them.

But he remained where he was until a sharp cracking sound startled him. He could not know that it was only a tree contracting in the cold. In his fright and hunger he sped back to the camp. It was no longer a camp. All that he found were the remains of campfires and worn-out items the Indians had left behind.

As he wandered through what was left of the once-busy campsite, he found that he not only missed his mother. He longed to see Gray Beaver again. He would have been glad to have had the squaws shouting and throwing stones at him. He would even have welcomed the sight of Lip-lip and the troublesome pack of dogs.

When morning came, he was desperate for the companionship of men. Remembering the direction the Indians had taken, he began to run after them. All that day and all through the night he ran, never stopping during a period of more than thirty hours. He followed along the Mackenzie, hoping to catch sight of Gray Beaver and the rest of the tribe.

White Fang's frantic search could have been in vain, since the Indians were on the opposite

bank of the river. But something happened
that would bring man and wolf together again.
Gray Beaver was told by Kloo-kooch that she
saw a moose drinking from the river on the
other side. So the family crossed the river, and
Gray Beaver killed the moose. Because it was
late, the family camped on the side of the river
White Fang had been following.

Coming at last to the camp, White Fang
lowered his body and crawled toward the fire

where Gray Beaver sat. He expected to be beaten, but it did not matter. The freedom he had desired did not satisfy him. He belonged with man, and he was willing to pay whatever price that relationship would cost.

Gray Beaver stared at him. Then, as White Fang drew within reach, he saw the Indian's hand move upward. It seemed that the beating he had expected was about to begin. But as he looked up, he saw that Gray Beaver was only reaching for a piece of meat. And then he was offering it to White Fang. The wolf hesitated, then took the meat gratefully.

In a few moments his stomach was full. He lay by the fire, close to Gray Beaver's feet. No more would he seek freedom from man's rule. He was home, and this was where he would stay.

CHAPTER 8

In the Service of Man

❦

In the snow-covered Wild, when winter's
hazards limit a horse's effectiveness, dogs
serve in teams pulling men's sleds. To the
cry of "Mush!" they make their sure-footed
way over hills, through valleys, and down
frozen streambeds. With their aid men are
able to hunt, to travel and trade, and to perform other actions in conditions that might
otherwise make it impossible.

Among the breeds of dogs that are used for
pulling sleds are Siberian huskies, Alaskan
Malamutes, and Samoyeds. The word "mush,"
by the way, comes from a French word mean-
ing "to fly." These dogs are all strong enough

113

that they almost seem to fly across the snow while drawing a sled carrying several hundred pounds of food, blankets, and equipment.

Wolves can also become sled dogs. During White Fang's first winter with Gray Beaver, he learned what was involved in being part of a sled team. He actually helped pull a sled driven by Mit-sah. Gray Beaver used the older dogs for his own larger sled, while his son used the puppies in drawing a much smaller one.

When he was first harnessed to the sled, White Fang accepted it quietly. He had committed himself to serving man, and this was part of that service. Even before he was a sled dog, he had seen the older dogs working in this way. He knew what would be expected of him.

His team consisted of six puppies. The Indians arranged their team differently from the way white men did. Bill and Henry, the men known to Kiche, lined their dogs up single file, one following behind another. Mit-sah, after the example of his father and his race, arranged them in fanlike fashion. This evenly distributed the weight each dog would pull.

The Indians' arrangement had one other advantage. The dogs, being at different distances from the sled, were connected to it by lines of differing length. This kept them away from one another. A journey by this sled was less likely to be interrupted by a fight between the team members.

The dog that had the longest line and ran in front of the others was in a troublesome position. The team members behind him thought that he was always running away from them. This caused them to hate the leader and to become bolder in attacking him when they were free from the sled.

Mit-sah put Lip-lip, who was now his dog in this less-than-honorable place of leadership. Mit-sah had watched quietly during all of the time Lip-lip had brought misery to White Fang.

Now the young man had an opportunity to turn the tables on the bully, and he did so.

What happened as a result of all this was that Lip-lip rather than White Fang became a target of the other dogs. He could no longer lead the others in warfare against White Fang. Now when he was not pulling the sled, he stayed close to Gray Beaver, Kloo-kooch, or Mit-sah. If he strayed away from them, he was open to attacks by the pack.

Lip-lip's downfall gave White Fang a chance to become the pack's leader. He continued instead to keep himself apart from the dogs. His only contact with them was through fighting. And since he could now meet them in one-on-one combat, he was a consistent winner. Indeed, he became something of a bully himself. If any dog ate his share of the meat too slowly, White Fang would hurriedly eat his own and then snatch away the other dog's as well.

He only showed a spirit of faithfulness and willingness toward Gray Beaver. He no

longer questioned this man's power over him
or thought of escaping again into the Wild.
But in his relationship with his master there
was still no affection. Had Gray Beaver
stroked or spoken to him in a kindly way,
White Fang might have developed some
affection for his master. But Gray Beaver continued to use harshness rather than kindness
with White Fang.

His earlier dislike for human children was
unchanged. Children were cruel in pulling his
ears and tail and fur. Once a very small child
almost poked his eye out. And in a village at
Great Slave Lake, on a journey with his human
family, he had an experience with a child that
caused him to react with violence.

The problem developed when he saw a
boy chopping the frozen meat of a moose
with an axe. In every village White Fang had
visited, the dogs had been allowed to eat the
chips of meat that flew in every direction during such chopping. But as he began to claim

these chips for himself, the boy picked up a club and chased him through the camp.

Since he was unfamiliar with the camp, White Fang did not know where to flee. Running between two tepees, he found himself facing a high earth bank. He had no way of escape as the boy closed in on him, preparing to strike with the club. Without thinking of the consequences, White Fang leaped, knocked the boy into the snow, and buried his fangs in the hand that held the club. Then, knowing he was in trouble, he fled to where Gray Beaver was.

The boy's family soon arrived. They insisted that White Fang be severely punished. Gray Beaver, Kloo-kooch, and Mit-sah had already learned something of the circumstances of the attack. It was clear to them that the boy was the one who was at fault. Therefore, they did not back down one bit in defending White Fang.

Later that day the boy stirred up trouble again. Mit-sah had gone alone to the nearby

woods to gather firewood. The boy showed up with some of his friends and began arguing with Mit-sah. The argument soon turned into a fight, with the local boys ganging up on Mit-sah and beating him badly.

Arriving at the scene, White Fang saw what was happening. He leaped angrily into the midst of the conflict. After about five minutes the bleeding and bruised boys had fled, and Mit-sah was safe. The young man went to his father and explained how White Fang had rescued him. In a rare act of gratitude Gray Beaver saw that the wolf was given as much meat as he could eat.

In such ways White Fang was bound ever closer to Gray Beaver and his family. He may not have known love for his master, but his loyalty in service grew stronger day by day.

Winter came to an end, and with it the days of pulling Mit-sah's sled. White Fang was now one year old. With the exception of Lip-lip, he was the largest of the dogs his age in the camp. Of course, it was still stretching matters somewhat to refer to him as a dog: He looked like a full-blooded wolf. The one-fourth strain of dog in his bloodline did not affect what he looked like.

As far as his acceptance of a dog's relationship with man and a dog's duties in man's service, he was a dog. He was still something of an outcast from the standpoint of the other dogs. But that did not matter to him. He was able to defeat almost any of the dogs his age in battle. And upon his return to the camp he found that even the grown dogs were no longer as frightening to him as they had once been.

One day early in the spring the Indians killed a moose and butchered it. White Fang received as his portion a hoof and part of a shinbone, with a generous amount of meat attached. He was privately feasting upon this, when an older dog named Baseek appeared. In months past White Fang had run away in fright whenever Baseek uncovered his fangs.

But now, when the older dog tried to take away his food, White Fang slashed viciously at him with his own fangs.

For a moment the two animals faced one another, with the shinbone lying between them. White Fang remembered his fear of Baseek and almost backed off, letting the older dog have the food. But when Baseek regained his boldness and went for the meat, White Fang forgot his hesitation and attacked.

He tore into Baseek's ear, then knocked him off his feet. With a sudden thrust to the throat, he could have killed his older opponent, but he did not do it. He allowed Baseek to regain his footing, and then rushed in to rip twice at an exposed shoulder. Baseek tried to strike back, but White Fang dodged and laid open his opponent's nose. Finally, acting as though the meat were not that important, Baseek gave up the fight and slipped away.

This victory seemed to make White Fang an equal among the grown dogs. As with the puppies, he formed no friendships with the older dogs. But they now treated him with respect. They knew that it was not wise to bully him.

With his wintertime labors in front of the sled and his springtime growth in importance among the camp dogs, White Fang had almost forgotten his mother. But one summer day he saw to his surprise that she was in the camp. And with her was a new litter of puppies.

He was glad to see her, but she did not share his gladness. In Nature's plan a she-wolf is made to forget her cubs of past years, giving her full devotion to her newborns. So she greeted White Fang with snarls and sharp strikes with her fangs. When he tried to sniff at one of her puppies, she became especially violent and tried to drive him away.

Her behavior toward him puzzled him. And then he was suddenly aware that it did not matter that she had forgotten him. He did not need her any more. He had grown

strong enough that he could get along without her.

This awareness was made clearer when she struck at him one more time. He allowed himself to be driven away. Had it been a male coming at him with fangs bared, he would have fought back. But even if Kiche was not his mother, he would not have faced her in battle. Wolves observe a kind of law that Nature has written in their minds, a law that forbids males from fighting with females.

With his mother now fading from his memory, he could not remember how she had saved him from famine when he was a tiny cub. Her hunting had brought just enough game to preserve his life and hers. Since that time he had experienced very few times of hunger. The humans had shared with him the fish they caught and the moose, caribou, and other beasts they killed.

During the third year of his life, the Indians had great difficulty finding food for themselves, much less their dogs. A terrible famine began in the summer, lasted through the following winter, and continued until another summer arrived. It brought weakness and death to the tribe. Hunger took the lives of the very young and the very old. The Indians were so desperate for food that they ate the leather of their moccasins and mittens. They also used the weakest of the dogs for food.

With no food for them in the Indian camp, some of the dogs escaped into the woods. White Fang was among these. The other dogs either starved to death or became food for wolves, because of their inexperience with the Wild. But White Fang survived. He was able to regain the hunting skills he had learned as a cub. At times he caught squirrels and tiny wood mice. On occasion he fought with other preying animals, such as weasels, and feasted on their flesh. And, unaware that he was following in his father's footsteps, he once robbed a rabbit snare—one that Gray Beaver himself had set.

He even ate his own kind. Finding a young wolf by itself, he ran it down, killed it, and ate it. Some time later, he narrowly escaped a wolfpack that pursued him. Drawing upon his cleverness and superior quickness, he circled around behind them and picked off one at the back of the pack for another meal.

It was during this time away from the camp that he saw his mother for the last time. She was occupying the lair in which White Fang had been born. In the lair was a new litter of cubs, none of which would survive. Kiche snarled a warning at him as he approached, and he turned away from her as though she were a stranger.

The famine was almost over when he met another animal he knew. It was Lip-lip, who had also left the camp to hunt for himself. They came face-to-face at the base of a high bluff, and immediately the old hatred flared.

All of those occasions when Lip-lip had bullied him came to mind. White Fang felt a growing fury within him. He was not hungry, for he had eaten well during the previous week. But he was ready to kill, for here was an old enemy who would have killed him, had there been a chance to do so.

Like most bullies, Lip-lip was not so eager to fight now. He was no longer larger than White Fang. And he was less successful as a hunter, so he was not in as healthy a condition. Furthermore, he did not have the pack of dogs that had joined him in camp in his early attacks on White Fang.

The fight was brief and one-sided. As Lip-lip tried to back away, White Fang rushed at him and bumped Lip-lip hard enough to knock him over. His throat was exposed, and White Fang sank his teeth deep into it. In a few moments Lip-lip was dead, and White Fang resumed his journey.

Soon afterward he came to the Indians' camp. He saw right away that there was food in it. The famine was at last over. Trotting into camp he found the tepee of Gray Beaver. The man was not there, but Kloo-kooch was. She gave White Fang a glad welcome, presenting him with a freshly caught fish. With a full stomach he lay down to await Gray Beaver's arrival.

CHAPTER 9

The Enemy of
His Kind

~~~~~~~~~~~~~~~~~~~~~~~

White Fang had known a great deal of
abuse and very little kindness.
Human beings had beaten him,
shouted angrily at him, and chased him away.
Dogs had challenged him and fought him. His
own mother, once a provider of kindness and
care, had become a stranger to him. It was not
surprising what results all of that produced in
him.

As deep as his hatred was already for his
own kind, it soon became deeper. Mit-sah was
responsible for this, since he decided to make
White Fang leader of the sled team. That task
had once led to the downfall of Lip-lip. In

White Fang's case it meant that any hope was gone that he could have become friendly with the other dogs.

Now it was White Fang who was out in front of the rest of the team. Now it was he who seemed to be fleeing from them as they pulled the sled. That was especially difficult for him because he had beat every one of them in battle. He yearned to be able to turn back on them from his position at the front and punish them with his fangs. He quickly found that was unwise. Mit-sah carried a thirty-foot-long whip of caribou gut, and he would snap its stinging lash in White Fang's face any time he would dare turn his head.

Mit-sah contributed in one other way to this deepening of hatred. He used a trick he had previously used with Lip-lip in order to increase the other dogs' ill-will toward their leader. He gave, or sometimes merely pretended to give, more food and other special favors to White Fang. This made the other dogs jealous of their leader. They ran faster and pulled harder when they thought they were pursuing their hated sled leader.

Of course, when the dogs were in camp and free from their sled duties, they were still unable to outfight him. They were more willing than ever to try because the impression that he had been running away from them made them bolder. But he quickly reminded them in every battle that he was superior in strength and movement.

Most of the time he did not enjoy the advantage of meeting them one-on-one. As it had been during his days as a cub, the dogs usually came at him as a pack. They were able in this way to preserve their own lives and to deliver a few effective slashes upon him. But one thing they were never able to do was to knock him off his feet. Had they done that, one of them may have succeeded in making a fatal thrust to his throat. But he was too quick and sure-footed to allow that to happen.

His reputation as a fighter was growing among the Indians in many villages. This reputation received quite a boost when he was five years old. Gray Beaver took him on a lengthy journey with visits in villages on the Mackenzie, the Porcupine, and the Yukon Rivers. The dogs in these places did not know him, so several attempted to meet him alone. The result was that he killed every challenger, while scarcely ever receiving a wound.

This journey brought him and his master at last, in the summer of 1898, to Fort Yukon. It was a time of excitement. The discovery of gold had brought thousands of visitors to the area. White Fang saw, for the first time in his life, men who were white. And it did not take him long to determine that these men were more powerful than the Indians. One of the ways that power could be seen was in the places where they lived. Instead of tepees, the white men had broad log houses in which to dwell.

Gray Beaver was excited by the presence of the white men who had come seeking gold. He had brought with him large numbers of furs, mittens, and moccasins, hoping to sell them at a handsome profit. But he was amazed at how well he did. A one hundred percent profit would have gone beyond his hopes, but he was selling at a one thousand percent rate. He decided to remain at Fort Yukon as long as he had goods to sell.

With little to do, White Fang roamed the fort and the surrounding area. He spent quite a bit of time by the river bank, watching steamers arrive and depart. In this way he saw more and more of the white men and became more and more impressed with them.

The white men brought dogs with them, and these did not impress him. They were weak, stupid creatures that would slip away from their masters and choose to take him on. He was easily able to defeat them and kill some of them.

He was clever enough to avoid killing them while their masters were present. As soon as he had delivered the deadly strike, he would hustle away. The pack of dogs belonging to other Indians would rush in to finish destroying the victims. The white men would see these dogs and wade into them with clubs, axes, and other weapons. On one such occasion a white man drew a revolver and shot six dogs before the sound of firing frightened the rest of the pack away.

During this time White Fang lived for this fighting. When Gray Beaver needed him, he was ready to do his master's bidding. But for now he took pleasure in doing battle with and destroying the dogs from the south. They came on shore, promptly recognized him as an enemy, and rushed at him. But their size and strength was never a match for his speed and cleverness.

CHAPTER 10

The Misnamed Master

Human beings do many peculiar things. One strange practice is to call one another by names that simply do not fit. For example, a fellow who weighs in at better than three hundred pounds may receive the nickname "Tiny." Another who wears a continual frown on his face may be called "Smiley." Still another man with a quiet, mild-mannered spirit may be known as "Tiger."

Among the white men who lived in Fort Yukon was one who wore the nickname "Beauty." Both in physical appearance and in personal character he was anything but beautiful. Beauty Smith was first of all a small man with an even smaller head. In contrast to this his face was quite broad, and he had an oversized, sagging jaw. He also had large, yellow teeth; eyes that were also yellowed; and dirty yellow hair that grew in clumps on his tiny head.

The main feature of his character was his cowardliness. That was mixed with a strong dose of greed. When he first learned of White Fang's ability as a fighter, he began to dream of how much money he could make if he owned that wolf. And he began to plot ways to convince Gray Beaver to sell the wolf to him. As a coward, he looked for ways to accomplish his aim that would not require any courage.

As part of his plotting, he made several efforts to win White Fang's friendship. However, the wolf made it clear that he was not interested in such friendship. White Fang sensed something evil in this man. He was determined to stay as far away from him as possible.

Beauty Smith was not discouraged by White Fang's obvious hatred of him. What he had planned for this animal did not depend on any affection between the wolf and his new master. He decided to put his plot into motion.

He paid a visit to Gray Beaver at the Indian's camp. White Fang was lying near his master when the visitor arrived. When he saw who it was, he moved to the edge of the camp and watched. Beauty Smith and Gray Beaver engaged in a lively discussion, and at one point the white man gestured in White Fang's direction. The wolf did not want to be noticed by this evil man, so he slipped off into the woods.

Gray Beaver told the white man that he was not interested in selling his "dog," as he now called him. The animal was too valuable as a sled dog. Furthermore, he was a powerful fighting dog. The Indian was obviously pleased that he owned an animal with such a far-reaching reputation as a killer.

Beauty Smith went away unsuccessful in this first attempt to buy White Fang. But he was prepared for the likelihood that his plot would take time to succeed. In the following days he returned several times to Gray Beaver's camp. On these occasions he took a black bottle with him. He was sure that whiskey could accomplish what simple persuasion could not.

Gray Beaver began to develop a thirst for the whiskey. He also began to spend his money carelessly so that he could satisfy his craving for the drink. Soon he used up all he had earned from his trading. The remaining goods he possessed also went into purchasing whiskey. Finally, he had nothing left with which to buy the drink he was desperate to have.

This was the circumstance that Beauty Smith had foreseen in his plot. He raised again the matter of buying White Fang. To make his appeal stronger he offered not dollars, but bottles, as the purchase price. Gray Beaver was no longer able to resist.

A few days later the deal was completed. It was on an evening when White Fang was resting in the camp, relieved that the evil man was not present. He made no protest when Gray Beaver staggered over to where he lay and tied a leather thong around his neck. But nothing else happened. The Indian sat down beside his dog and took frequent drinks from one of his bottles.

About an hour later Beauty Smith appeared. White Fang was now his property, and he wanted to touch his property. As he approached and lowered his hand, the wolf snarled a warning and then snapped at the hand, barely missing it. Gray Beaver struck him sharply on the side of the head, and he crouched in submission on the earth.

This punishment was not enough for his new master. The evil man walked a short way into the woods and returned with a thick branch he could use as a club. Gray Beaver handed the end of the thong to him, and he pulled it tight around White Fang's neck. He began to try to lead the wolf out of the camp. White Fang responded by rushing at him. But Beauty Smith was ready for this. A vicious blow with the club sent the wolf sprawling on the ground.

White Fang was wise enough to know that further resistance was useless. He allowed himself to be led to the fort. On the way he made his displeasure known by snarling softly. But he saw that his new master was keeping the club handy, so he did not try to attack again.

He was easily able to escape. With Beauty Smith in bed asleep, he clamped his teeth on the thong, quickly cut it, and hurried away to Gray Beaver's camp. As far as he was concerned, the Indian, and not this hated white man, was still his master.

But his loyalty to Gray Beaver did not affect the Indian. Once again Gray Beaver tied him with the thong. On the following morning the

Indian once again gave him to the evil man.
Beauty Smith was determined to show White
Fang who his master was now. Using both a
club and a whip, he gave the wolf the worst
beating he ever received in his life.

In this matter Beauty Smith demonstrated
his cowardly character at its worst. A man who
would run from a fair fight had a beast before
him that was helpless. Of course, White Fang
was not helpless in the sense that he lacked
the strength to defend himself. But he had
yielded himself to man's power. Because of
this he would accept whatever man saw fit to
do to him. Only this kept him from striking
back as his new master brutally beat him.

Once again Beauty Smith dragged him back
to the fort; once again the man tied him tied
up for the night. This time, however, he was
tied so that a stick prevented his getting at the
leather thong.

He had seen other dogs change owners,
and he knew what was involved in that. To

run away from Beauty Smith was an act of disobedience. He understood that. Yet his faithfulness to Gray Beaver was not something he could easily give up. The Indian had betrayed him by selling him to this evil man, but he was still determined to return to Gray Beaver.

This time it took much more effort to free himself. He had to gnaw at the stick throughout the hours of the night until he finally broke through it. Early morning had come when he trotted again into Gray Beaver's camp. Once more the Indian tied him with a thong. Beauty Smith arrived and administered an even more severe beating than before.

When they reached the fort, he was secured with a chain. His teeth were powerless to break through that. He saw that a large staple held the chain to the wall of the fort. For a time he struggled and strained in an effort to pull it loose. But soon it was clear that he would not escape this time.

He did not know that Gray Beaver was out of reach. On the morning after the last act of giving up White Fang, the Indian left on the long journey back to the banks of the Mackenzie River. White Fang would never see him again. Now he belonged to a master who had plans for him that would have nothing in common with pulling a sled.

Beauty Smith knew that the men who came to Fort Yukon were eager for entertainment. Some of these men had come with a measure of wealth; others had been successful in their quest for gold and gained wealth in the Yukon. Either way, they had money they would be willing to spend on entertainment. And a fight between a powerful dog and White Fang was the kind of spectacle that was sure to draw these men with their money.

The evil master knew from the beginning that White Fang could win him a large amount of money. He was clever enough to see that his wolf had a combination of physical

strength and skill in fighting that no dog could beat. By this time White Fang was five feet long, weighed over ninety pounds, and was all muscle and bone. He represented all the best features of the wolf, by way of his father, and of the dog, by way of his mother.

Beauty Smith learned how to prod the wolf into a rage as a way of preparing him for combat. The master kept White Fang in a pen. He would stand outside and poke at him, taunting him to build up his anger. He also discovered how White Fang hated to be the object of scorn and laughter. He used this knowledge to stir up the beast even more.

White Fang's first fight as a possession of Beauty Smith was against a mastiff. This large and powerful-looking dog seemed to onlookers more than a match for the wolf. But White Fang struck a quick blow to the mastiff's neck. Then he swiftly dodged every one of the dog's lunges toward him, while frequently leaping in to slash with his fangs. There was soon no question that he was the winner. The mastiff's owner dragged his badly wounded dog out of the pen, while White Fang's master beat him back with a club.

It was the start of a very profitable ownership for Beauty Smith. Each time White Fang was about to fight, his master placed sizable bets on him. And he never failed to collect from those who bet against his wolf. This was true even when White Fang's challenges were increased. Once he was required to fight three dogs, one right after another. On another occasion he fought a full-grown wolf. His toughest test, however, came when two dogs were put in the pen with him at the same time. He killed them both, but only after narrowly escaping death himself.

His reputation as "The Fighting Wolf" was well-established by the time he left Fort Yukon. He was going on a trip to Dawson with his master by steamboat. The journey was a miserable one for him. First of all, he hated being confined in the pen. While Gray Beaver was his master, he had been free to move about and explore things that made him curious. But even that had been taken away from him.

There was one other aspect of his journey that added to his misery. On board the steamboat that made its way up the Yukon River were passengers who had heard about him. They crowded around his pen, prodded him with sticks, and laughed at him. He had developed an intense hatred of Beauty Smith for such behavior, and he felt the same kind of hatred for these other white men.

Dawson was a city that had grown rapidly following the gold strike. Many men who had come here were hungering for entertainment. At first Beauty Smith merely put him on display in the cage as the famous fighting wolf. Men were willing to pay fifty cents in gold dust for an opportunity to see him. Of course, he had to put on a good show, so his master kept him stirred up in a rage by jabbing him with a sharp stick.

Soon he was back into the round of regular fights again. These had to be arranged carefully to keep them from the attention of the Northwest Mounted Police. The Mounties frowned on gambling activities such as these. The fights were therefore held away from town in the woods and always at night. White Fang's opponents were of various breeds and sizes. He fought Mackenzie hounds, Eskimo and Labrador dogs, huskies, and Malamutes.

In all these encounters he maintained his ability to keep his footing. His opponents tried their best to strike him in order to knock him over on his side. But he was so swift he kept them from succeeding in this. And he had fighting experience that none of his foes could match. From his battles with Lip-lip and the pack of puppies to his contests with the animals sent into his pen, he had learned all the tricks of effective fighting.

The time came when no more dogs were matched with him. Instead, he fought with wolves that the Indians trapped for just that purpose. Once he did battle with a full-grown female lynx. She was every bit as quick and powerful as he. She had the same advantage his mother had once fought to overcome: the combination of flashing teeth and ripping claws. In this fight his experience was the only difference between victory and death.

After this victory he fought no more until the following spring. He was regarded as unbeatable. Then, a man brought in an animal that had not been seen before in that region. It was a bulldog, a short, compact dog with powerful jaws and a reputation for persistence in a fight. Its owner thought it would make a worthy opponent for White Fang. Beauty Smith had not made much money of late from his fighting wolf, so he was eager to arrange the match.

By the evening of the fight many of the area's citizens knew of it and were eagerly anticipating it. A huge crowd gathered in a woods outside of Dawson and placed their bets. Human beings like to see an "unbeatable" champion go down to defeat. So many of the spectators bet their money on Cherokee, the bulldog, and began to cheer him on.

When the bulldog's owner pushed him into the pit with White Fang, the wolf looked over this strange new foe. Unlike the many dogs he had faced before, Cherokee did not appear eager to fight. He merely stood in the center of the pit, blinked at White Fang, and wagged his tail in response to the spectators who were urging him to the attack.

Cherokee's owner knew how to get him into a fighting mood. Bending over the dog he began to rub the hair on his shoulders in the wrong direction. In a few moments Cherokee started to growl softly. Then the growl rose louder. Finally the owner gave his bulldog one more push toward the wolf.

White Fang waited no longer. With a swift move he closed on the bulldog and ripped his flesh open behind one ear. Then, again and again over the next few moments he slashed at his foe. Cherokee, however, seemed unaffected by these wounds. He merely chased after the wolf with a single-minded determination to catch him.

Each animal was puzzled by the other's behavior. White Fang could not understand how the bulldog could take so much punishment without a single yelp of pain. He never seemed to make an effort to defend himself. He just kept moving after the wolf in spite of bleeding from various gashes in his body. And Cherokee was troubled that White Fang was constantly dodging his advances and staying out of his reach.

The battle could have been quickly finished had White Fang been able to get at Cherokee's throat. But the bulldog stood too low to the ground and was too heavy to

161

be knocked over. His powerful jaws made any thrust toward his throat a dangerous move.

Somehow White Fang had to get at the throat in order to finish this opponent. So he kept making unsuccessful attempts to bump the bulldog off his feet. At last he made one such attempt that brought a result, but not what he wanted. In completing a rush upon Cherokee, he struck the bulldog in such an awkward manner that he lost his own footing. For the first time in a fight he went down on his side. He was able to regain his footing, but as he did, Cherokee moved in and clamped his jaws onto his exposed throat.

Fortunately the bulldog's teeth were not able to close in on the blood vessel. But he was near enough that White Fang panicked for his life. He spun around; he shook his body; he struggled to free himself from the fifty-pound weight clamped to his throat. But none of his efforts worked.

Cherokee was not about to let go of this grip on the wolf's throat. He clung to White Fang with the stubborn determination for which his breed is known. And he was patient in waiting for the opportunity to make his hold more secure and, finally, more deadly.

As his strength began to give out, White Fang used every move he could think of to try to free himself. He fell over again, but with Cherokee moving on top of him, he was able to rip at the underside of the bulldog's body with the claws on his hind paws. This would have worked, but Cherokee was able to shift his position to avoid the claws.

Slowly Cherokee was moving his grip, getting perilously close to the blood vessel. White Fang would already have been killed if it had not been for the loose skin and thick fur on his neck. This formed a kind of roll in Cherokee's mouth and helped shield White Fang's throat from the tightly clamped teeth.

Those men who had bet on the bulldog were close to celebrating a victory. But Beauty Smith had one last hope of saving his wolf and his money. Stepping up to where White Fang could see him, he pointed a finger at the wolf and began laughing. It was an effective trick, for White Fang felt a fresh surge of anger. He struggled to his feet again and began to whirl and to shake his body.

But this could not last. His remaining strength was soon gone, and he fell over once more. Cherokee shifted his grip slightly closer to the blood vessel. The end of this fight and the end of White Fang's life seemed only minutes away.

CHAPTER 11

Rescue and Release

The discovery of gold in the Yukon Territory had not only brought great numbers of treasure-seekers to the region. It also brought experts who could determine where and how to dig mines, and who could also check on the safety of existing mines. Weedon Scott was one of these experts. He had left behind a family and the comforts of a home in California to work for a while in the Yukon.

On the night of the fight between White Fang and Cherokee he and his musher, or sled driver, were returning from inspecting a nearby mine. As they followed their sled and dogs on the trail to Dawson, they saw a crowd gathered at the edge of the woods. Curious to see what was happening, they stopped their dogs and moved in among the spectators.

Scott was not surprised by what he saw. He knew that animal fights were an acceptable form of entertainment in this region. But seeing the hopeless situation of the wolf with the bulldog gripping his throat stirred deep emotions within him. He was a lover of animals, and he did not care to see any creature mistreated.

He would probably have walked away from this disgusting scene if something else had not happened at this point. Beauty Smith, realizing that his fighting wolf was on the brink of losing, charged into the ring and began kicking the dying creature. Some in the crowd voiced their protests over this, but they did nothing else to stop it.

His eyes suddenly blazing in anger, Scott shouldered his way through the rest of the crowd and entered the ring. Beauty Smith was ready to deliver another kick when Scott's fist smashed into his face. The evil master tumbled backward into the snow.

Scott turned to the crowd and scolded them for their cruelty and cowardliness. Out of the corner of his eye he saw Beauty Smith get to his feet and come up behind him. As the most cowardly person present, the evil master had no intention of taking a swing at the intruder. But Scott did not know that, so he spun around and landed a second blow to Beauty Smith's face, again sending him sprawling into the snow.

The newcomer then turned his attention to the dogs. With the help of Matt, his musher, he tried to pry open Cherokee's jaws and free White Fang. That did not work. Next he tried striking the bulldog on the head with several solid blows. But Cherokee only wagged his tail in response. He seemed to be saying that he was just doing his job by clinging to White Fang's throat.

Scott turned to the crowd. "This fight is over," he announced. "But we need someone else's assistance to free the wolf."

A few of the spectators were leaving. Others stayed close, but they avoided Scott's gaze. No one stepped forward to help.

"Why don't we try to use your revolver to pry open the bulldog's jaws?" Matt finally suggested.

Scott nodded, drew out his revolver, and guided the barrel between Cherokee's jaws. Then he pushed upward with all his strength. He could hear the gun's metal grating against the teeth, but the grip on White Fang's throat remained as firm as ever.

Scott noticed that someone from the crowd was standing beside him. But he quickly found it was no helper.

"That's my bulldog," the man said in a warning tone. "You make sure you don't break his teeth."

"If you're not going to help us, just move back out of our way," Scott answered. "I don't

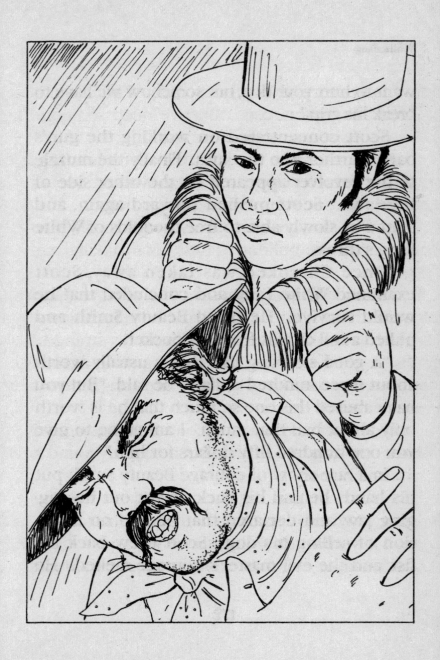

want to hurt your dog, but somehow we have to break his grip."

Scott concentrated on working the gun's barrel farther into the jaws. Finally the muzzle of the revolver appeared on the other side of the jaws. Scott pushed upward again, and Matt was slowly able to free the folds of White Fang's throat.

Once Cherokee was taken away, Scott examined White Fang and concluded that he would survive. He faced Beauty Smith and pulled a roll of bills from his pocket.

"A good sled dog like this is usually worth about three hundred dollars," he said. "But you have abused this one so much that he is worth only about half that much. I am going to give you one hundred fifty dollars for him."

In a rare show of courage Beauty Smith put his hands behind his back, thrust out his sagging jaw, and declared that he had no intention of selling his dog. Scott drew back his fist, and the evil master's courage melted. He whimpered something about taking the money under protest as he accepted the bills Scott held out to him.

Then, with Scott's fist lowered, and having moved a few feet away from the man, Beauty Smith issued a threat:

"You just wait until I get back to Dawson! I'll have the law on you!'

"If you say one word about this in Dawson," Scott answered coolly, "I will personally have you run out of town. Do you understand that?"

Beauty Smith could see that his cause was lost. Not only was Scott threatening him, but he was aware that some in the crowd were laughing at him. With one last glance at the fighting wolf, he slipped away from the scene.

Weedon Scott and Matt carried White Fang back to their cabin. Over the next few days they nursed the wolf-dog back to health. But if they expected the animal to be grateful and

cooperative, they soon found they were wrong. White Fang had learned to hate both beast and man, and that hatred was unchanged.

After a few days of laboring to win White Fang's trust, Scott had grown very discouraged. He sat on the step of his cabin one morning and discussed the problem with Matt.

"I have just about decided it's hopeless," Scott confessed. "That animal is a wolf, and there is simply no way to tame it."

Matt had been observing Scott's efforts without comment during the preceding days. His back was turned to White Fang, but he lifted his hand and gestured with his thumb toward the animal.

"Whether you call it a wolf or a dog, one thing is for sure: he has been tamed already." When Scott raised his eyebrows as if to question that statement, Matt added, "Look at those marks across his chest."

Scott looked more closely and exclaimed, "You are right, Matt! He must have been a sled dog before Beauty Smith became his owner."

Matt suggested turning White Fang loose and seeing what happened. Scott protested that he might run away. But since nothing else had worked, he agreed to Matt's suggestion.

The dog musher was going to take no unnecessary chances. Before he approached White Fang, he picked up a club. Both men noticed how the animal trained his eyes warily on the club. It was clear that he knew he dared not take on Matt, so long as the man had that instrument in hand.

White Fang could not understand what was happening. Was he about to be beaten? He snarled a warning as the man's hand reached for his neck, but the nearness of the club in the other hand kept him from snapping. In a moment the hand drew back after removing the chain that had been fastened to his collar.

For the first time in months White Fang was actually free. During the time Beauty Smith was his owner, he had constantly been either in a pen or on the end of a chain. The only exceptions had been those brief periods when he was fighting some other animal. Now he was free, but he was not certain what to do with his freedom.

Cautiously he walked toward the far side of the cabin. Then he turned and moved back to within a few feet of the men. They could see he was puzzled by this turn of events, and he was clearly suspicious of what was going to happen next.

"Keep an eye on him, Matt," Scott said. "I'm going to try something else." He went into the cabin for a minute and returned with a piece of meat.

Matt laughed. "You think you can win him over with kindness—is that it?"

"We've tried everything else. Let's see what happens with this." He tossed the meat

toward White Fang, but the suspicious animal
jumped away from it. From a safe distance he
eyed the human's apparent gift.

One of the men's sled dogs, named Major,
had been watching this scene. It was too
much of a temptation for him to resist the
meat lying on the ground, so he sprang upon
it. In a flash White Fang was upon him, slashing his throat and striking a deadly blow. Matt
rushed in and lifted his foot for a kick at the
wolf-dog. That was a mistake, for White Fang's
teeth sank into the extended leg. When they
pulled away, Matt's trousers were torn, and
blood appeared through the shredded cloth.

In the meantime Scott had drawn out his
revolver. He was ready to use it on White Fang
when Matt cried out to him.

"Don't do it, Mr. Scott! The poor dog's had a
rough life. We have to give him a chance now."

"But it looks more hopeless than ever,"
Scott answered. "Major is dying, and you've
been injured, too."

"Major got what he deserved," Matt said. "He tried to take away another dog's meat. And as for me, I should have known better than to try to kick him."

"He cannot be tamed," Scott insisted. "It would be better for him and safer for us and our dogs to kill him."

Matt was not about to give up. "Let's give him one more chance," he said. "If he does not change, then I'll kill him myself."

As he put his revolver away, Scott nodded to Matt. "All right. We'll give it one more try."

Scott approached White Fang with careful steps and soothing words. The wolf-dog did not run away, but he remained suspicious. After all, he had killed this man's dog and had wounded his human companion. It seemed likely that some form of punishment was coming.

As White Fang crouched down, his eyes watchful, his body tense, the man began to lower his hand. The wolf-dog snarled a warning, but the hand kept coming closer. Suddenly, he struck with lightning quickness, and Scott, with a cry of surprise and pain, drew his torn hand away.

It was Matt who picked up a weapon this time. But as he brought his rifle to his shoulder, Scott told him not to shoot. Matt was about to argue that it needed to be done. However, both men's attention was drawn to the wolf-dog's snarling as he gazed at the rifle pointed toward him. He had run to the corner of the cabin, where he waited, ready to take cover if Matt put his finger to the trigger.

"That is one intelligent dog!" Scott exclaimed. "He knows what a gun is, and he is ready to do whatever he can to avoid being shot. We have to give intelligence like that a chance."

Matt leaned the rifle against a nearby wood pile. White Fang stopped snarling as soon as the action was taken. Then Matt snatched up the rifle again and raised it to his shoulder.

With a final violent snarl the animal darted behind the cabin.

"You are right, Mr. Scott," Matt said solemnly. "That dog is too intelligent to kill."

The Triumph
of Love

We can never fully know what kinds of suffering another being has endured. Perhaps we know someone who has a very gloomy and grouchy outlook on life. That outlook may have resulted from grief or disappointment that we know nothing about. On the other hand, a person with a cheerful and sunny disposition may carry some terrible burdens beneath the surface. It is important that we try to understand other people, how they think and why they act as they do.

There was no way Weedon Scott could understand all of White Fang's experiences.

When he interrupted the wolf-dog's cruel fight with the bulldog, he could only guess concerning White Fang's earlier life. The countless beatings by his evil master and many times he had been poked, prodded, and laughed at turned White Fang into a creature controlled by hatred.

On the day following his slashing of Scott's hand White Fang was expecting punishment. Of course, he was free to escape if the man approached with club or whip. He could have run away during the preceding night. But he remained close to the cabin, waiting to see what would happen.

When Scott came out of his cabin on this morning, he carried no weapon. And when he spoke to the wolf-dog, there was no threatening tone, no hint of anger. Still, White Fang had learned that men were capable of deception. Apparent acts of friendship could turn to cruelty. So he continued to be wary even though something told him he could trust this man.

The man went back into the cabin after spending several minutes merely talking to the animal. When he reappeared, he sat down where he had been before. He extended his hand, showing that he held a small piece of meat. White Fang eyed it with interest, but he kept his distance. After a few moments the man tossed the meat to him. He sniffed it, waited for some evil trick to happen, and finally ate it. These same steps were repeated several times.

White Fang realized that the man intended for him to come and take the meat directly from his hand. Little by little he moved closer to that hand. He never took his eyes off the man, nor did he stop growling deep in his throat. But he at last accepted the meat from the man's hand. As he ate, he stayed alert for the punishment the man might be plotting.

The man's kind voice was working a strange effect on him. He was experiencing feelings he had never felt before. The desire to trust this man was stronger, but a part of him was fighting that desire.

And then he saw the man's other hand, reaching out toward him. Was the punishment finally to be administered? He snarled and flattened his ears, but he did not intend to snap unless that hand caused him pain. When it touched the hairs of his head, it did not bring pain, but a curious sense of pleasure. He continued to growl softly, even as the hand stroked and petted.

Matt came by as this was happening. His mouth fell open, and he stared at the surprising scene for several moments before speaking.

"I never thought I'd see this!" he exclaimed. "Every time I think we are about to convince that wolf we are his friends, he starts growling and snapping at us again."

"It just takes time and patience," Scott explained. "I believe he will learn to trust me."

"I wouldn't be so sure about that," Matt replied. "You may find out yet that you've been a fool in trying to tame that beast."

Matt's concern would soon vanish. That day was one that he and Scott would later remember as the turning point. White Fang would still snarl and make threatening gestures, especially toward Matt. But he soon learned to like Weedon Scott.

He had known two previous human masters. Gray Beaver had been good to him in many ways, and he in turn had served the Indian faithfully. Beauty Smith had been an evil master, and White Fang had done his bidding with a heart filled with hatred. With Weedon Scott he found an entirely different kind of master. Here was one who was kind, one who dealt with him gently.

He liked Weedon Scott. As a result, he gave this man a kind of loyalty that neither of his previous masters could have won. He made himself the guardian and protector of his master's property. It took time for him to learn the difference between friends and enemies, honest men and thieves. He was aware that anyone who came sneaking up to the cabin, who moved softly and silently, was likely not an honest person. He dealt fiercely with such visitors.

As far as his master's dogs were concerned, he knew he must not kill them. However, he did take on each of them in a series of early fights and soundly defeated each one. That served to show them that he was to be respected and obeyed. They learned that lesson well, and for a long time he had no trouble with them.

It took a little longer to work out a peaceful relationship with Matt. He did not forget the musher's kicking at him and pointing the rifle at him. Still, Matt also seemed to be a possession of his master. Usually it was Matt who gave him his food. But White Fang knew it was actually his master's food, so he gladly accepted it. But he did not want Matt touching him, and he worked for Matt only when the master made it clear he should do so.

White Fang went from liking Scott and serving him with loyalty to the point of genuinely loving him. He showed his love in quiet ways. The dogs might run up to Scott and bark happily and wag their tails when he returned from being away. That was not the wolf-dog's way, but he loved the man every bit as much as they did.

He soon learned that love has a painful side. A few months after his rescue from

Beauty Smith, he found out what happens when the object of one's love is taken away.

He had seen Scott packing his belongings in his luggage, but he did not understand what that meant. His master left the cabin, but he had done that before and then returned later. This time, however, he did not return. Anxious and perplexed, White Fang spent that night on the cold front step of the cabin, waiting to hear the familiar step and voice of his master.

Scott was gone several days. During his absence Matt became very worried about the wolf-dog. He was not eating, and he was not willing to work. The sled dogs had sensed that he was not in a fighting mood, and they had been able to get away with abusing him. He ran from them rather than turning his fangs upon them.

Matt was so concerned about White Fang that he wrote to Scott. He explained that he did not know what to do about the problem.

"I'm afraid that wolf is going to die, if you don't get back soon," he concluded.

On the evening of Scott's return White Fang was inside the cabin. When he heard the footsteps he had been waiting to hear, he began to whine. Matt was not even aware that Scott was approaching. But the door opened and his master entered the cabin. White Fang began to wag his tail in delight, just as any good dog would upon seeing his master again.

Scott greeted White Fang with his kindly voice. Then he squatted down next to the wolf-dog, rubbed behind his ears, and ran gentle fingers along the fur of his back. Desperate to find some way to express his own love and joy at his master's return, White Fang did something his old wolf nature would never have permitted. He thrust his head in between his master's arm and body and snuggled there in perfect contentment.

"Well, look at that!" Matt exclaimed. "I'm the one who feeds him and protects him from the dogs. He hardly pays any attention to me. But just as soon as you walk in the door, he comes to life again."

Scott winked at Matt. "I guess he knows who saved him from getting shot."

In the days that followed, White Fang returned to what had become his normal life. He ate his food happily. When called upon to work, he did so willingly. And if the dogs challenged him with their newfound boldness, he promptly put them back in their place.

One night, soon after Scott's return, he and Matt were about to head for bed, when they were startled by noises outside the cabin.

"That's White Fang snarling at something or somebody," Scott said.

Matt reached for his riffle, as he heard a man's cry of pain. "It sounds to me like it's a somebody. And that wolf must be giving that somebody a rough time."

They snatched up a lamp and hurried outside.

The light of the lamp revealed a man lying on his back in the snow. He was desperately trying to protect himself from White Fang's attack. His arms were folded across his face, and he was struggling to get over on his side. The wolf-dog had torn his clothing into rags, from top to bottom, and had also ripped into his flesh. Blood was everywhere.

When they succeeded in dragging White Fang away, Matt helped the wounded man to his feet. As the lamp revealed his face, they saw it was Beauty Smith. At about the same time they noticed two objects lying in the snow. One was a steel chain for holding a dog, and the other was a stout club.

There was no need to punish Beauty Smith for attempting to steal White Fang. The wolf-dog had already taken care of that. Matt merely laid a firm hand on the man's shoulder, turned him around, and pushed him back up the trail.

CHAPTER 13

Good-bye
to the Yukon

The pain of separation—we have all felt it. When a friend moves away from our community, or when a family member leaves home for a long time, it hurts. This is a common human experience, but it is also something that animals feel. We handle this pain of separation by thinking about something else, but animals do not understand this kind of approach.

White Fang's master had left him once. It had been a gloomy, painful experience. And now he sensed that it was about to happen again.

Weedon Scott's work in the Yukon was finished. It was almost time to return to his home in California. He had given serious thought to taking White Fang with him. But over and over one question troubled him: "What can I do with a wolf in California?"

He had debated the matter with Matt. One by one he listed the problems: White Fang would surely kill his neighbor's dogs. Those neighbors would take action against Scott over the loss of their property. Eventually they would demand that White Fang be put to death. Matt outwardly agreed with all these arguments. At the same time, he spoke in such a way as to make Scott feel guilty over his plans to leave the wolf-dog behind.

One evening he discussed the matter with Matt. "There is no escaping the truth," he said. "White Fang will surely kill the neighbors' dogs. The neighbors will come to me and demand that I do something about my killer wolf. Finally it will reach the point at which they will want him put to death."

"You're absolutely right," Matt answered. "But of course that wolf will also die if you leave him here. He'll stop eating again. Before long he'll be so weak the dogs will kill him."

Scott was already feeling guilty about leaving the wolf-dog behind. White Fang had begun to show his awareness that Scott was leaving soon. He would lie outside the cabin door, whining for hours at a time. Occasionally they would hear him sniffing at the door as he reassured himself that his master was still inside.

Finally it was time to pack. When White Fang saw, through the open cabin door, his master's luggage with clothing in it, he knew he would be left behind again. That night he kept Scott and Matt awake with his mournful howling.

Scott finished his preparations for leaving in the morning. To make his departure easier, he called White Fang into the cabin. He took a few moments to rub and stroke the wolf-dog and to say his final good-bye. Then he walked out the door, closed it, and locked the animal inside. As he headed toward Dawson and a waiting steamboat, he groaned at the terrible howling coming from inside the cabin.

Soon he was on the deck of the steamboat, saying good-bye to Matt. The two men had shaken hands, and Matt was about to leave the boat, when Scott cried out.

"It can't be! Matt, look down there on the dock and tell me that isn't White Fang."

Matt shielded his eyes from the morning sun and peered at the dock. "It's him, all right. But how did he get out of the cabin?"

They hurried to where the wolf-dog was sitting and watching them. A closer look gave them the answer to Matt's question.

"Look at those fresh cuts along his muzzle," Scott said.

"He jumped through a window!" Matt replied. "We should have thought of that. He

wanted to stay with you bad enough that he wouldn't let a little glass stop him."

This show of love and loyalty was too much for Scott. Matt was looking for a way to tie the animal, so that he could lead him back to the cabin. But Scott reached out to shake Matt's hand.

"Good-bye, Matt," he said. "You don't need to take him back to the cabin. He's coming with me."

"Are you sure?" Matt asked.

"I'm sure I can't leave him here," Scott answered. "I'll write to you and tell you how he gets along."

And so White Fang left behind the life he had known. No more would he feel the snow and cold of the Wild. No longer would he exert his strength as part of a team drawing a sled across the snow. Never again would he do battle with wolves or lynxes or weasels.

He was no longer a cub in a world he was eager to explore. But he still found satisfaction in learning. And there was much more to learn! The long journey on the steamer led at last to the great city of San Francisco. For the first time in his life he looked up at buildings that reached into the very heavens. He saw automobiles and cable cars. Then there were the people, countless human beings coming and going on the busy streets.

The excitement he felt in seeing all this was mixed with a sense of confusion and fright. All the people and things constantly in motion made him feel a bit dizzy. It made him appreciate even more the master he trusted and loved. Not once did he take his eyes off the man who had rescued and released him from a life of misery.

The stay in San Francisco was brief. The journey continued by train. White Fang was separated from his master during this trip. He had to be chained in the baggage car. If he could not be with his master, then he would commit himself to guarding his master's luggage. So well did he

do this that no porter was able to touch the luggage until Weedon Scott appeared.

When he left the baggage car, White Fang was relieved to see that the noisy city was gone. He was in open country again, but nothing like the country he had once known. Here it was sunny and warm, calm and peaceful.

The master led him to another object with wheels, which had horses harnessed to it. Near this carriage stood a man and woman. Upon seeing his master they hurried to him, and the woman put her arms around his neck in an embrace. Thinking that she was somehow harming his master, he snarled a terrible warning to her.

Scott silenced the wolf-dog and reassured his parents that White Fang would not harm them. Deciding that it was as good a time as any to teach the animal about his family, he embraced his mother again. When White Fang reacted again in a threatening manner, Scott again silenced him.

Once the humans were in the carriage, the horses began to pull it away from the train station. As it rolled along the road, it raised a cloud of dust. White Fang dashed along behind, ignoring the dust. At times, he would rush up near the horses as if to warn them to be careful with their duty of transporting his master.

It took only fifteen minutes for the carriage to reach the fine home occupied by the Scott family. Intent on his master's safety, White Fang could not notice the broad lawns surrounding the place, the golden fields nearby, and the distant sun-splashed hills.

But he was about to notice one feature of his master's house. As he followed the carriage through the gateway and into the grounds, he saw an angry sheep dog coming right at him. He might have ignored this animal, but it moved between him and the carriage. So he charged toward it, fangs bared.

He never completed his attack. As soon as he saw the sheep dog was a female, he pulled up and tried to turn away. Many of the features of his old wolf nature had changed, but this had not. Males did not attack females, and he was not about to break that unwritten law.

The law, however, did not affect her. Her breed regarded the wolf as a deadly enemy of the sheep they guarded. So she sprang on him and clamped her teeth into his shoulder. He retreated and then tried to circle around her. But she continued to stay between him and the carriage.

As the carriage moved farther away and disappeared around the house, White Fang began feeling desperate. His great aim in life was to remain close to his master, and this sheep dog was preventing his doing that. He would not attack her with his teeth, but there was something he could do. Turning suddenly upon her he threw his shoulder against hers and sent her rolling out of his way.

She recovered quickly, but all she could do was to chase him as he sped around the house and found the carriage. He was happy to see his master again as he stepped down out of the carriage. But he did not see another attacker's approach. A deerhound came rushing at him, struck him on his side, and caused him to tumble over.

White Fang scrambled back on his feet and was ready to move in on the deerhound and seize its throat to kill it. But the sheep dog arrived just in time to save the deerhound's life. She rammed the wolf-dog just as he was making his spring. Once again he was knocked off his feet.

The master and his father reached the scene at this point and separated the animals. Scott held White Fang firmly and stroked him to calm him. He spoke soothingly to the wolf-dog, but in a lighthearted manner:

"Old boy, you just met Collie, our sheep dog, and Dick, our deerhound. I guess they did not give you a very friendly welcome. In all your life you have been known only once to

have been knocked off your feet. Now they have tumbled you twice in thirty seconds."

Other women had come out of the house. They threw their arms around the master's neck as his mother had done earlier. White Fang was beginning to recognize that this was a harmless act, so he did not snarl at them. When they turned and started to move in his direction, both the wolf-dog and his master warned them not to touch him.

The master and his family started up the steps to enter the house. Dick was on the porch. He began to growl as White Fang followed his master. The wolf-dog growled back at him.

"I have an idea," Scott's father said. "We will take Collie inside. Your wolf and Dick can stay out here and fight it out. Once the fight is over, they'll probably be friends."

"The only problem with that," Scott answered, "is that White Fang will have to show his friendship by attending Dick's funeral. Dick would be dead in one or perhaps two minutes."

The older man looked a bit shocked. After a moment he said, "All right, then. Collie will stay outside. The wolf is the one who will come inside."

CHAPTER 14

Learning a New Life

Sierra Vista—that was the name of White Fang's new home. It belonged to his master's father, Judge Scott. It was home to several other dogs besides Collie and Dick. After the first day, most of those dogs looked upon White Fang as an acceptable resident of Sierra Vista. He had been taken by the human beings inside the big house, and that was a sign he was to be accepted.

The one dog that did not look upon White Fang as an acceptable newcomer was Collie. She was constantly troubling him during the days after his arrival. Since White Fang's nature forbade him from fighting back, he could only protect himself from her regular attacks. His years of experience in battle, combined with his quickness, made these defensive efforts successful.

Working out his relationships with the dogs was simple compared to learning about the human beings who lived at Sierra Vista. To him they all belonged to his master. That meant he had to learn to get along with them. First of all, there was Judge Scott and his wife. They were the actual owners of Sierra Vista, but to White Fang they would always rank below his master.

Three other women were a part of the family circle. These were Scott's two sisters, Beth and Mary, and his wife, Alice. Their habit of clutching the master in their arms was something White Fang could not understand. But the master seemed to enjoy it, so the wolf-dog soon gave up his suspicion regarding it.

Weedon and Alice Scott had two children, four and six years of age. The younger was a boy, also named Weedon; the older was a girl named Maud. White Fang's experiences with children had not been happy ones, so he was slow in trusting young Weedon or Maud.

The master was insistent that White Fang learn to accept the children's touches. If the wolf-dog growled at their approach, the master would cuff him as a way of showing displeasure. It was a light cuff, but since White Fang was anxious not to displease his master, any such cuff made a deep impression on him.

It took quite a bit of time, but White Fang learned to like the children. He didn't enjoy their efforts at petting as much as the master's, but he did take pleasure in the touches of their hands. He would never respond to their childish voices in the way he did the master's, but he did like hearing those young voices.

Besides the family members, Sierra Vista was populated by a number of servants. Most of these people had no interest in making

friends with White Fang. Instead, they feared him and kept their distance from him. And that arrangement was exactly what he wanted.

He did have one rather violent encounter with one of the servants. White Fang made the mistake of feeding on Sierra Vista's chickens. He of course had grown up as a hunter and killer of wildlife for his food. On a couple of occasions he saw stray chickens that had escaped from the yard where they were kept. It seemed only natural to pounce on them, kill them, and eat them. And he was pleased to find that they were very tasty.

On the second of these occasions, one of the men who groomed the horses saw him killing and eating the chicken. Armed with a buggy whip the groom rushed forward to punish White Fang. The wolf-dog, stung twice by the whip, leaped for the groom's throat. The suddenly frightened man lifted his arm to protect his throat and his forearm was ripped open to the bone.

The groom was in danger of losing his life to the angry wolf-dog. But Collie arrived in time to save him. She moved between White Fang and the groom, giving the man the opportunity to escape into the stables. After a few moments of snapping at White Fang, she forced him to retreat.

This created an uncomfortable situation for Weedon Scott. First, he had to defend White Fang for his attack on the groom. The man should never have used the whip, he explained. Instead, he should have come directly to White Fang's master and reported the incident.

As for killing the chickens, Scott pointed out that the wolf-dog was capable of learning to leave them alone. But before he could be taught, he had to be caught in the act.

He was caught in the act three days later. But it was an act far more serious than his master had anticipated. White Fang found a way into the house where the chickens roosted. During the night he killed fifty of them. And when the master brought him the following morning to the place where the dead chickens were laid out, the wolf-dog seemed proud of his killings. He certainly showed no signs of guilt over doing what was his nature to do.

All Scott had to do was to perform three simple steps. First, he spoke with sternness and anger to White Fang. Then he held the wolf-dog's nose down to sniff at the slain chickens. As he did so, he cuffed the animal more firmly than usual. It was an effective lesson for White Fang never again raided the chicken's house.

Scott's efforts to cure White Fang of his chicken-killing were not convincing to his father. "Once an animal has developed the habit of killing other animals, there is no changing him," Judge Scott declared.

"Let's work out a little test," Weedon suggested. "I'll lock White Fang in with the chickens for one complete afternoon. Then, for every chicken he kills, I will pay you one dollar gold coin."

Judge Scott agreed to this. Beth and Mary, overheard this discussion. They whispered something to one another, and Beth asked, "Could we make a suggestion?"

"I'm suspicious of those smiles you are both wearing," said the judge, "but tell me what you have on your minds."

Mary responded, "If White Fang has to pay a penalty, Beth and I think you should also accept some kind of penalty, Father. It's only fair."

Judge Scott pondered that for a moment. He turned to Weedon and said, "That sounds reasonable to me. What kind of penalty should I agree to?"

"How about this?" Weedon said to his father. "When we let White Fang out of the chicken yard, we will see what has happened. If he has not harmed a single chicken, you will

have to apologize to him in the presence of the family. It will be just as though you were sitting at your judge's bench. You will say to him very solemnly, 'White Fang, you are smarter than I thought.' And you will do this once for every ten minutes he spends in the yard."

With these arrangements worked out, Weedon Scott let White Fang into the chicken yard. The family members found hidden places to watch the wolf-dog. But he did nothing. He slept for a while. He got a drink of water from the chickens' trough. Finally, he leaped to the roof of the chicken house and then down to the ground outside the fence.

A little later the family gathered on the porch. Judge Scott faced White Fang and, with all the solemnness he could muster, he paid his penalty. Sixteen times he said, "White Fang, you are smarter than I thought."

As time passed, White Fang learned which animals he was to leave alone and which ones he could kill. The animals that belonged to his master, his family, and other human beings were forbidden. These included dogs, cats, turkeys, and rabbits, as well as chickens. But the creatures that lived in the wild, such as jackrabbits, squirrels, and quail, were game he could kill.

He did struggle to keep from attacking other human beings' dogs, particularly those dogs that would attack him. At a certain crossroads he and the master passed on the way to town were three dogs that always challenged him. For a long time White Fang was able to keep them away by snarling at them. But even at a distance they would bark and yelp at him, and he did not like that.

One day the dogs made their usual rush at him. He again warned them away. This time, however, the dogs' owners urged them on to a full attack. The master pulled his carriage to a halt as this was happening.

"Go get them!" he said to White Fang.

The wolf-dog had learned to control himself so well that even that word of encourage-

ment did not immediately move him. He looked questioningly at the master.

"They have pestered you long enough," the master said. "Now go, eat them up!"

White Fang sprang into action. In a few minutes two of the dogs were dying, their throats torn open. The third one tried to escape, but White Fang easily caught up to him, dragged him down, and killed him.

The dogs' owners could not protest. They had urged their dogs on against White Fang. Their dogs had died as a result. The men had learned it was not wise to fool with Scott's fighting wolf, and they spread that word throughout the entire region.

As White Fang moved into the latter years of his life, he enjoyed an easy, generally care-free existence. Once he had been a hunter. Then he had labored as a sled dog. Then he had served the hated Beauty Smith as a fighting wolf. Now he had no work to do. His only responsibility was to heed the will of his master, and that never involved any hard work.

His life was also free from fear. Once the dogs of the region and their owners learned to respect him, there was no animal he had cause to fear. No animal, that is, except Collie. And even toward her he felt no fear, but he did grow weary of her constant pestering.

The master made many efforts to create a friendship between the sheep dog and the wolf-dog. But Collie would have none of that. She never forgot the incident of the chicken-killing. If White Fang made any move that suggested he might pounce on a pigeon or chicken she would bark and snarl. He learned that the best way to silence her was to lie down and pretend to go to sleep.

Collie tried to make his life miserable, but the moments he spent with the master made it all bearable. The master would romp and wrestle with him. On many occasions the master would go out on horseback and invite him to run alongside the horse. And this was not really work. Even at this point in his life, White Fang could run fifty miles in an afternoon without tiring.

On one of these afternoons he was able to express his loyalty to the master in a special way. They had journeyed out to a distant portion of the Sierra Vista property. The master decided it was time to teach his young horse how to open and close gates without the rider's dismounting. The horse merely grew more nervous as time after time he was led up to the gate to close it.

Since the lesson was not succeeding, the master finally turned the horse toward home. But the animal was still nervous. When a jackrabbit suddenly dashed in front of him, he reared up and threw Weedon from his back. The master fell awkwardly to earth. As he rolled away from the horse's flying hooves, he felt a sharp pain in his leg. He realized the bone was broken.

White Fang was ready to punish the horse for injuring his master, but he halted when he heard the master calling to him.

"I need your help, old fellow," Weedon Scott said, his eyes reflecting the pain of the broken leg. "You must run home and tell my family to come. I have no paper or pencil to write a note. So it is up to you to convince them that I need their help. Now go!"

Among these words White Fang could understand only "home" and "go." He knew that the master wanted him to go home. But he hesitated to leave his master here by himself.

"Go home!" the master insisted. There was no disobeying such a sharp command. White Fang hurried down the broad pasture, heading toward the house.

He found the family on the porch. The children saw him first and ran to greet him.

Ordinarily he would have been glad for their attention. Now, however, he had an urgent message to deliver in some way. He growled at Maud and young Weedon. When they failed to get out of his way, he darted between them and caused both of them to fall.

Alice Scott watched this with a dark frown on her face. She called to the children, comforted them, and warned them not to bother White Fang.

"That animal makes me very nervous when he is around the children," she told the other family members. "I am afraid that someday they will do something to make him angry, and he will turn on them."

Judge Scott nodded his agreement. "I know Weedon thinks he can be trusted, but he is still a wolf. And I just hope the children are nowhere near when he decides to act like a wolf."

White Fang was desperately trying to find a way to deliver his message. He did a few little anxious turns in front of the judge, whimpering as he did. But the judge merely commanded him to go away and lie down.

The wolf-dog turned to Alice. He seized the hem of her dress in his teeth and pulled. The fabric ripped, and the sound of its ripping was accompanied by Alice's frightful screaming.

"I think he is going mad!" Judge Scott's wife exclaimed.

"I think he is trying to tell us something," Beth said. She had taken the role of White Fang's defender whenever Weedon was absent.

In his desperation to deliver his message, White Fang did something he had never done before and would never do again. He burst into a fit of barking.

Alice and her mother-in-law spoke at almost the same time: "Something has happened to Weedon!"

They left the porch and followed him out into the pasture. He did not bark again. He simply ran on ahead, stopped until they caught up, and then ran ahead of them once more. At last they reached the place where Weedon lay.

After this event, the people of Sierra Vista regarded White Fang with greater respect and affection. Even the groom, whose whip attack had brought on the wolf-dog's vicious reaction, admired him. The judge, however, continued to insist that a wolf could never be anything but a wolf and could not be entirely trusted.

When the master was able to ride again, White Fang eagerly resumed his running alongside the horse. There was coming a day when he would let the master ride out alone. The reason for this was Collie, but it was not because of one of her assaults.

About the time of White Fang's second winter at Sierra Vista. he noticed a change in

Collie. At one time she had attacked him constantly, but now she approached him in more of a playful spirit. Earlier her teeth had been sharp when she sank them into his shoulder. Now her thrusts at him were mere nips.

One afternoon he found himself facing a difficult decision. The master had saddled his horse and was almost ready to ride. As White Fang waited, Collie appeared. She gave him a playful nip and then began running for the woods. He hesitated for a moment, looking at the door through which the master was about to come. Then he hurried after Collie. The master would ride alone that day, and he understood why his wolf-dog did not accompany him.

Even deeper than his love and loyalty to his master, White Fang felt a calling that drew him after Collie. His mother, Kiche, and One Eye had once felt it and had run together in the Wild as mates. Now he had found his mate.

CHAPTER 15

Guardian
of the House

A judge holds an awesome responsibility. The fate of men and women accused of crimes depends on his absolute fairness in his courtroom. When his court determines if someone is guilty, he must decide a sentence that fits the crime. Many times judges have mistakenly sentenced an innocent person because of false testimony or poor evidence.

In Judge Scott's last days on the bench a man by the name of Jim Hall appeared before him. Hall was a known criminal, who had twice before been convicted of crimes. But when he stood before Judge Scott, it was for a crime he had not committed. The judge was

237

not aware that some of the testimony given had been false. He sentenced the man to fifty years in prison.

Before Jim Hall was taken to San Quentin Prison, he announced his intentions to gain revenge on the judge for the severe sentence. It was the kind of threat Judge Scott had heard many times before, and he did not worry about it.

The convicted man's hatred grew while he was in prison. An especially brutal guard fanned the fires of hatred, until one day Jim Hall attacked the guard and killed him with his bare hands. For this he was placed in a cell for hopelessly hardened criminals. Over a period of three years he lived in continual darkness and silence.

His rage finally led him to attack and kill another guard. Somehow he was able to escape his cell. Then, by slaying two more guards, he escaped from prison. He took all the weapons of the dead guards with him.

During the days that followed he killed and wounded many other people. Farmers with their shotguns, businessmen with their rifles, and lawmen joined in the manhunt. On a few occasions they caught up with Hall, but he was always able to get away after a deadly exchange of gunfire. And then at last he disappeared completely.

The news of all these incidents made most of the residents of Sierra Vista quite anxious. But Judge Scott did not seem concerned. He told his family that Jim Hall was probably either dead or heading in a direction that took him farther away.

Weedon Scott's wife Alice was terribly worried. She feared for the judge's safety if the criminal were to show up at Sierra Vista. She feared as well for her own children. And so, each night after everyone was asleep, she secretly let White Fang into the big hall downstairs. Then she arose early in the morning to let him out before any family member awoke.

One night White Fang awoke and realized that a stranger was in the house. His nose picked up the unfamiliar scent. His ears heard unusual movements. Without making a sound the wolf-dog arose and walked softly toward those movements.

He reached the foot of the great staircase. His eyes were accustomed to seeing in the dark, and he was able to see a man who was about to go up the staircase. White Fang did not, of course, know who this man was. However, he knew the stranger did not belong in the house. And he was about to go up to where the master and his family were.

White Fang crouched silently and sprang. His forepaws struck the stranger's back, and his fangs sank into the flesh on the back of his neck. The two of them crashed to the floor. The wolf-dog aimed his next thrust at the man's throat. As he rushed in, the sound of revolver shots rang in his ears, and he felt bullets tearing through his body.

In spite of the searing pain, he clamped his fangs into the exposed throat and completed the fatal attack. Then he rolled over on the floor. He lay there, the blood pouring from his wounds.

The lights came on. Weedon Scott and the judge came down the stairs cautiously. Each held a revolver in his hand. The stranger was lying faceup on the floor at the foot of the stairs, obviously dead.

"It's Jim Hall!" Judge Scott exclaimed. "I guess he did get his revenge. But how did White Fang get in here?"

"I have no idea," Weedon said. He knelt on the floor to examine the wolf-dog. "He's still alive, but barely. Hall shot him, and he's lost a lot of blood. I doubt that he will survive."

"He will if I have anything to do with it," the judge declared. "That animal probably saved my life! He may have saved the life of every person in this house. Now we have to do our best to save his life." As the judge spoke, he went to the telephone. He called his own surgeon and briefly explained what had happened.

The surgeon soon arrived and worked on White Fang for an hour and a half. The entire family, except for the children, gathered to hear the results of his examination.

"He has a broken hind leg," the surgeon began, "which is the least of his injuries. Three of his ribs are fractured, and one of them has pierced a lung. He was shot three times, and the bullets went clear through him. Because of that he lost almost all of his blood." The surgeon paused to let all that sink in, then concluded. "I would give him, perhaps, one chance in ten thousand of making it."

Judge Scott remained hopeful. There seemed nothing he would not do for the wolf-dog now. He called for another doctor to come from San Francisco, and he announced he was ready to hire a trained nurse. Beth, Mary, and Alice promptly told him he would not need a professional nurse. They would

give White Fang all the attention he would need to make him well.

The next few days were anxious ones at Sierra Vista. But White Fang survived and slowly began to regain his strength. He pulled through. It was not because of the skills of the doctors or the loving attention of the women. And it was not because of the tender concern of his master and the newfound care of the judge. All of those contributed something, but his survival depended more on the fact that he was a creature of the Wild. The strength of his breed and the toughness he had inherited from Kiche and One Eye made the difference.

On the day that his last bandage and plaster cast were removed, he was given a new title. It was Alice who first said it: he was now "the Blessed Wolf." The other women quickly adopted it, and soon even Judge Scott was using it.

As soon as he was rid of the bandages and casts, White Fang was ready to try to stand up and walk. He was still quite weak, so it took a great deal of effort to get onto his feet. At last, to the cheering of his admirers, he was up and moving.

With the surgeon's approval "the Blessed Wolf" was led outside. The family surrounded him as he slowly made his way across the lawn. His strength grew with each step. By the time he reached the stables he was moving with a minimum of difficulty.

At the doorway to the stables an amazing sight greeted him. Collie lay there. Around her were six puppies, frisking and stumbling under her watchful eye. She was not pleased to see him, and she made that clear with a warning snarl. But one of the women put an arm around the sheep dog's neck as Weedon used his toe to guide one of the puppies toward White Fang.

He was at first suspicious of the little bundle of fur. As he watched it curiously, it stretched out its neck and touched noses with him. Then it licked his muzzle, and he licked its face in return. The family members cheered once again.

White Fang was feeling a little weak again after his walk. He lay down, and the rest of the puppies moved awkwardly toward him. Collie did not like it, but they were his puppies, too. He closed his eyes and allowed himself to enjoy their bumping and tumbling over him.